This book is dedicated to my mother, Arliss.

This is a work of fiction. Unless otherwise indicated, all the names, characters, places, events, and incidents in this book are either the product of the author's imagination or used in a fictitious manner. Any resemblance to actual persons, living or dead, or actual events is purely coincidental. This fictional piece of literature may contain content disturbing or offensive to some readers such as death, grief, abuse, and supernatural elements. Please note that it is not the author's intent to cause distress to any reader, but if you find any of these subjects triggering, please take note and proceed with caution. Remember to practice self-care before, during, and after reading. For more information, please go to: @vanessakramerauthor on Instagram.

Copyright November 2024 Virtue Publishing
Second Edition published November 2024

ISBN 979-8-9916277-2-6 (paperback)

1

"I'm leaving my big, American city to have fun in the English countryside," said no one ever.

I glanced once more at the last message I had sent. Still no reply. The night before our flight, I had stayed up until two o'clock in the morning talking to my best friend, Sarah. I was spending the whole summer in England with my parents and sister, and staying with family members I had never met before. I couldn't imagine a worse way to spend my summer. I was sprawled across my bed, sketching in my journal and listening to music, dreading the moment we had to leave.

Sarah's parents had made her get a summer job at the movie theater to pay for her new car. I would have given anything to trade her. I begged my parents to let me get a summer job since I had just turned sixteen. Working with my best friend, seeing movies for free, and having my own money; it sounded amazing. I had decided that it wasn't fair and I wasn't going. The car horn blared from outside. My mom was growing impatient. *Good*, I thought as I shaded in the cat I had been drawing.

"Time to go!" My dad yelled from the front door. I turned up my music louder. A wadded up piece of paper hit me suddenly in the head. I took out my earbuds.

"Hey, loser. Did you hear Dad? Everyone's ready to go."

I looked up to see my twin sister, Jo, standing in the doorway. She looked more like Dad than Mom. She had dark brown hair, brown eyes, and was blessed with straight teeth. I took after Mom, with dark blonde hair, blue eyes, pale skin, and crooked teeth. Luckily, my looks didn't completely reflect hers. I colored my hair hot pink, got braces, and after begging and pleading with my dad, got my nose pierced. Now, looking up at my twin who looked nothing like me, I decided to turn my "bitch mode" on.

"First off, get out of my room right now," I said. "Second, yes I heard Dad, and I don't care. I'm not going on this stupid trip."

I picked a piece of lint off my black Ramones shirt and went back to my drawing.

"As for the first thing, you can kiss my ass. As for the second, yes you are. Now come on before Mom comes and gets you. Do you want this 'stupid trip' to start off rough before we even leave the house?"

She had a good point, unfortunately. But that was Jo; the sensible intellectual. So what if she made straight A's and was taking all honors classes? Being intelligent certainly didn't help with her wet blanket personality. I'll admit it; she's the smart twin and I'm the creative, moody one.

I grabbed my journal and put it in my red and black carry-on bag. Then, I grabbed my guitar case and pushed past Jo.

"What about your other crap?" she asked.

"You've got two hands. Help me."

"What do I look like to you? Your personal bellboy? I'm the older twin. You can't boss me around."

"Being twenty minutes older than me doesn't mean shit," I smirked as I pulled my hoodie over my head. "Also, I'm the smaller twin. So you have to help me carry stuff."

"Pathetic," Jo scoffed and reluctantly picked up my suitcases.

Although I would never admit it, I would miss Jo when we went to different colleges. That is, if I even did go to college. I told my parents the only colleges that sounded good were art schools. They let me know that they had no intention of "wasting a college tuition on art."

"Well, it's about time!!" my mom said as we put my luggage in the back of the SUV (which I always say stands for "Slow and Useless Vehicle"). She was sitting in the front passenger seat next to her friend, Tina. Tina was nice enough to drive us to the airport so we didn't have to pay for a taxi or to park our car there all summer. I sat behind Mom with Jo squeezed in the middle, and Dad behind Tina.

"We could have driven to England by now!" Mom continued as we buckled ourselves.

"Talk to your other daughter about that," said Jo.

"There's no way you could've, like, driven to England," I said, pretending to sound as ditzy as possible. "It's totally across the ocean and cars can't go in water!"

"Abby, do you want us to just go without you?" my dad asked.

"Don't try and get my hopes up like that, Dad. I know I have to go."

"Watch it, Abby," my mom gritted her teeth.

Tina shifted her eyes awkwardly before pulling out of our driveway.

"Oh, I forgot something!" I said abruptly.

The car screeched to a stop.

"Just kidding," I grinned.

Before I could hear the next thing that came out of my mother's mouth, I put my earbuds back in and turned my music up as loud as I could stand it. I mimed to my mom that I couldn't understand what she was saying. It was fun to watch her mouth without having to hear whatever she was trying to yell at me. She eventually turned around but occasionally I would catch her glaring at me in the visor mirror.

The hour-long drive from Hoboken, New Jersey to JFK Airport seemed like it would never end. We weren't even on the plane yet and I was already bored. I tried to fall asleep, or at least close my eyes. But every time my eyes would start to flutter, Jo would elbow me in the ribs and quickly say sorry before smiling.

When we arrived at the airport, it took us another thirty minutes for Tina to find our terminal. After checking in all of our luggage, finding our gate, and actually boarding the plane, it was past five o'clock in the evening. My parents were smart enough to seat Jo and me away from each other. I sat with Dad while Jo sat with Mom. As the plane began down the runway, I started getting

5

a funny feeling in my stomach. *Am I forgetting something?* No, that wasn't it. I was nervous. I had never flown across the ocean before, and I wasn't looking forward to doing it. I wasn't looking forward to any of it. I grabbed my dad's hand tightly and closed my eyes, praying that the plane would shut down and we wouldn't have to go.

"It will be okay," whispered my dad. "Soon we'll be in the air and it will be night so you won't be able to see what we're flying over."

"Great," I breathed heavily. "Somehow being over the ocean in the pitch black doesn't make me feel any better."

"I'll close the shades," he said. "But I think it would make you feel better if you saw us take off."

"No thank you," I replied.

All of a sudden, the plane got a lot louder and accelerated. The funny feeling in my stomach rose to my throat. No way, I was not going to puke before we were even up in the air. I knew I shouldn't have had that supreme burrito for lunch. I could feel the plane tilt and rise off the ground. My grip grew tighter on my dad's hand. My ears popped from the pressure change and I suddenly was very sweaty. I should have taken my hoodie off. Once we were up in the air and level, the flight attendant announced that everyone could unfasten their seatbelts. I opened my eyes. People were getting up and walking around. Some were already falling asleep. But most were watching the featured movies in their seats, with headphones plugged in. Jo came up behind me and flicked my ear.

"How'd you like the take-off, sis?" she asked, chuckling.

"Bite me, Jo," I said, letting go of Dad's hand.

"Did you need something?" Dad asked. "Because if you're out of your seat just to torment your sister, you can march your butt right back to Mom."

I smirked as Jo walked back to her seat. On her way back, she stopped to check out a boy around our age on the other side of the plane. He was wearing glasses and reading a book.

"Joanna! Stop staring at that guy, you perv!" I yelled.

6

A couple of passengers stopped to look over at her, including the boy she was watching. Jo's eyes widened as she hurried to her seat, hitting her head on the overhead storage before ducking down. I smiled as I got my headphones out. I chose what movie I wanted to watch and pulled my journal and pencil out to draw. I was halfway watching a movie about a teenage girl falling in love with a boy who was secretly a demon when I started zoning out.

Tick-tock, tick-tock.

I opened my eyes and found myself in a dark room with no windows. No windows, *I thought.* How odd. *There were cobwebs on everything and the room smelled musty, like the old books at the library. I sat up on the bed I was laying on and reached over to turn on the lamp. The bed jiggled when I moved. The dim light made it easier to see the rest of the room. Everything looked old and strange. The wooden dresser was painted blue with all kinds of flowers on it. The crocheted doily on the end table had a purple phone laying on top of it. The Tiffany-style lamp next to the phone looked like stained glass. There was an armchair that was covered in squares of hideous fabric, making it look like a quilt. Another, smaller chair in the room seemed to be inflated plastic.* What a weird room.

Tick-tock, tick-tock. The grandfather clock in one of the corners kept calling out to me. I slowly got out of the wobbly bed and walked toward the clock. The wood was red-tinted and it had pictures of men on horses painted on it.

Tick-tock, tick-tock. My heart began to race, although I wasn't quite sure why. It was beating so loudly that I barely even noticed the creaking of the floor behind me. I was standing in front of the clock. My hand reached up, grabbed the handle, and pulled the door back. I wasn't expecting anything other than the pendulum and more dust. However, in the bottom of the clock was a small, black box. Why do mysterious boxes always have to be black? *I bent down to pick it up. There was a lock on it.* Of course.

"I know where the key is," said a voice from behind me.

I came to and was back on the plane. *I must have fallen asleep*, I thought.

"Wow, neat drawing," my dad said.

"Huh?"

I looked down at my journal and realized I had drawn, in great detail, the grandfather clock.

"It's from the dream I just had."

"Honey, you've been awake, drawing this whole time," he smirked. "You haven't been asleep."

"I'm going to go to the bathroom," I mumbled.

"Probably a good idea to get up and stretch," my dad smiled as he unbuckled.

I walked past my mom and sister and saw that they were both asleep. My mom's tray had several tiny bottles of wine on it. I rolled my eyes and headed to the bathroom. I stood behind an older woman who turned and smiled at me.

"All of these lavatories and there's still a queue," she said in a posh English accent.

"Mm, yes, quite!" I said in an over-exaggerated accent.

The woman gave me a dirty look as one of the doors opened and she hurried inside. I waited for the next door to open and realized how bad I had to pee. Suddenly, waiting for a bathroom wasn't so easy. A door opened and before the man could get out, I grabbed the handle.

"Excuse me!" I said as I pushed my way inside.

"Hey!" I heard him say as I shut and locked the door. I sat down and sighed. After I flushed, I checked out my reflection in the mirror. I gasped. My black eyeliner was smudged, making me look like a racoon. I was so relieved that my mom and sister were asleep when I walked by because at least one of them would have made a comment on my appearance. I grabbed a paper towel and ran it under the water. When I looked back at the mirror, the pale face of a woman appeared behind me. I shrieked as I whipped around to see that there was no one behind me. The lights flickered and my heart was pounding. I burst out of the bathroom and ran into the woman who had been waiting in line before me.

"Sorry!" I blurted before scurrying to my seat. My dad was already back in his place and I could see him watching me out of the corner of my eye.

"You okay?" he asked.

"Fine," I replied without looking at him.

"No one messed with you or anything? No one tried to touch you-"

"Dad!" I snapped. "No, gross! I said I'm fine. I'm just tired."

"Okay," he sighed. "We probably do need to try and get some sleep. Don't want jet lag."

I nodded and curled up against his shoulder. Trying to shake off what had happened in the bathroom, I let myself relax enough to finally fall asleep.

"Abby, wake up. Look outside."

My eyes fluttered open and I looked where my dad was pointing. The sun was coming up and we were over land again.

"What time is it?" I asked.

"It's about 6:55. You've been sleeping a while, honey."

"Pull the blinds back down," I grunted, pulling my hood down over my eyes.

Once I wasn't blinded by the sun, I sat up and looked around. Almost everyone was awake and putting their belongings back into their bags. I glanced at my dad while he folded up the newspaper he had been reading. He looked old and tired. He didn't used to look like that. With his new promotion, he had been spending a lot more time at work. He came home late often and sometimes skipped dinner. He used to have a lot more time for us. He used to have a lot more energy too. He was a fun dad to grow up with. Mom never wanted to play with us, but Dad was always up for it.

"How much longer?"

"We're getting ready to land in thirty minutes."

I pulled up the window blinds again slowly, squinting into the sun. As my eyes adjusted, I could see the land below us gradually get closer and closer, which was a great relief because I was starting to get a cramp in my butt. The landing was a lot smoother than the take-off, although I still tugged at my dad's shirt while the plane bumped on the ground. After we got off the plane, luggage in hands, we tried to find our rental car in the parking lot.

"The guy I talked to on the phone said the car was a blue four-door, but I don't see any," said my mom, looking around.

"Maybe that's it," I said pointing to a dark blue car at the end of the aisle.

"Abby, that's a black car," argued my mom.

"No, it's blue," I argued back.

"It's black."

"No, it's blue!"

"Can I help you, ma'am?" called a voice from behind the service desk. A nearly completely bald man hopped up and walked around the desk to us. He had an incredibly thick accent.

"Yes," my mom answered quickly, handing the man a piece of paper. "We're trying to find this car."

"Alright, it's the very last car on the right," he pointed to the very same car I had pointed to.

"That car is black," my mom said, obviously frustrated she had once again been proven wrong.

"No ma'am, I assure you. That car is blue. We have the descriptions of the cars straight from the dealers." My mom grabbed the keys while my dad signed the paperwork. She flopped down in the front passenger seat while my sister and I loaded the trunk with as many suitcases as possible. The rest went in the back with us. My dad got in the car and started it up. He flipped through radio stations for a moment.

"Just start driving," my mom said, turning off the radio. "We're already running late. You would think your company would have given you a better rental car than this."

"Just be grateful they wanted to pay for it," mumbled my dad.

"Only because they want you to work abroad," muttered my mom. "Blue, huh."

"Please, move on to something else," my dad sighed as he entered the address on the car's GPS. "I need to concentrate on where we're going."

"Good thing I turned the radio off then."

I don't know how my parents have stayed married as long as they have. They didn't really seem to like each other, let alone love each other. I sometimes wondered if my dad worked so much to avoid my mom. There had been some nights when my dad was still at work and the house was really quiet, I could hear my mom crying in her bedroom. I've thought about going in and checking on her, but the last time I tried, it didn't go so well. I've thought about talking to Jo about it, but it wouldn't do any good. Jo knows our mom is out of her mind; she just chooses to ignore it as best as she can. Not me though. I call my mom out on her craziness.

As we drove past the city landscapes, I began to wonder if we were actually staying in England.

"Um, Dad? I thought we would be staying in London," I asked.

"No!" he laughed. "We'll be staying about an hour away from London actually."

"Just when I thought this trip couldn't get any more lame."

Where else was there to go in England? I thought. *Where was Shakespeare from? What was the name of that stupid place? Why didn't I pay more attention in English class?*

"Are we going to Strutter up on Avalon?" I asked, hoping that was right. Jo started laughing. I knew that wasn't the name, damn it.

"Do you mean Stratford-upon-Avon?" asked Jo.

"Whatever," I glared at her.

"No," said my dad.

"Well are we going to Liverpool? That's where the Beatles are from, you know."

"No shit, Abby," Jo muttered. I flipped her off.

"I heard that," my mom scolded. "Watch your mouth. And no, Abby. We're not staying in Liverpool. Just wait until we get there."

I went back to listening to my music and laid my head back.

Help me. Find me. Help me. Find me. The same thing played over and over in my mind like a broken record. *Help me. Find me. Help me. Find me.* Suddenly, I felt like I couldn't breathe; like there were hands tightening around my throat. I shot forward, gasping loudly. Our car swerved on the road and everyone yelled.

"What the hell was that about?" My mom snapped.

"Jesus, Abby, you scared the crap out of me!" added Jo.

"You okay, kiddo?" my dad asked.

"I'm fine," I said, wiping my sweaty hands on my jeans. "Sorry."

My dad continued to glance back at me in the mirror occasionally as he drove.

"Weirdo," I heard Jo whisper.

Ignoring her, I looked out the window, watching as we moved further away from city life and out into the country. I wondered if I was starting to go crazy, like my mom. I thought about last November, when I ran away from home. My mom and I had gotten into a huge fight that had started over me coming home past my curfew. I knew I had screwed up, but my mom overreacted and told me I wasn't allowed to hang out with my group of friends anymore. As soon as she said it, I snapped at her.

"You can't keep me from seeing my friends!" I yelled. "I go to school with them! It's not like you can keep me from going to school!"

"No, but you will come straight home from school and you will not go out with them anymore. If your friends can't respect my rules then they're not your friends."

12

"You are so pathetic," I said. My mom recoiled as if I had hit her. "Just because you're miserable and have no friends doesn't mean you take mine away!"

"I'm done with this conversation," my mom threw her hands up before walking away.

"Sure," I scoffed. "Walk away instead of actually dealing with the problem. Mother of the year!"

My mom turned to walk back to me. Before she could get a word out, I cut her off.

"Are you sure you don't want a glass of wine before you keep yelling at me?"

Her hand hit my cheek so hard, my face turned away from her with force.

"You ungrateful little bitch!"

Suddenly, we both looked at the shape on the stairs and realized Jo was standing there. The three of us froze, unsure what to say or do. No one wanted to be the first to move. Finally, I pushed past my mom and stomped up the stairs. I paused briefly by my sister and said, "watch what you say. She's resorted to hitting now."

I made sure I got inside my room and shut the door before the tears started flooding out. I stood in front of the mirror on top of my dresser and stared at the red handprint on my cheek. I cried the entire time I packed my backpack and put my pajamas on. I laid in bed, thinking of my plan. At one point, my bedroom door opened and I heard Jo whisper my name. I didn't move. She closed the door and went to her room. A little while later, my door opened again. No one said anything or came into my room. Whoever it was just stood there for a bit and then left.

The next morning, I got dressed and ate breakfast, refusing to speak to anyone. Jo and I walked to school awkwardly.

"Are...you okay?" Jo asked quietly.

"No."

"You know she does love us."

"She sure has a screwed up way of showing it," I said rubbing my sore cheek.

"She wouldn't act like that if she didn't drink. And maybe went to therapy."

"Then Dad should make her stop drinking and start going to therapy!" I snapped.

"You can't make anyone do anything they don't want to do."

"I wish she wasn't our mom," I muttered.

"I sometimes wonder if she thinks the same thing," Jo said.

"Would you be okay walking home alone today?" I asked as we reached the school building.

"What?"

"I'm not going back," I explained. "I draw the line at being hit. And she called me a bitch. I'm done with her."

"Abby-"

"No, Jo! You might be okay with living in fear of her, walking on eggshells all the time. I'm not doing it."

"So you're abandoning me?" she asked, sounding hurt. "You're running away again?"

"You'd rather I stay and get treated like that?"

When she didn't respond, I smiled weakly and turned from the front door.

"Abby!" I heard Jo call. I didn't look back; instead I pulled my phone out to message my friends, Sarah and Motley and told them my plan.

Skipping school. Going to the mall. Never going back home. Meet me?

Even though I was freaking out, I tried to remain calm as I walked alone to the mall. The walk there took nearly the whole day since it wasn't close to the school. When I got there, I was so hungry, I immediately went to the food court. I only had enough money to buy a bag of chips. I sat at a table alone, eating my chips, and ignoring the phone calls from my parents and sister. Both Sarah and Motley said they weren't coming because they didn't want to get in trouble.

"Abigail?"

I looked up and a police officer was standing there. *Busted.*

Jo had immediately called my parents to tell them I was skipping school. When she asked Sarah if she knew where I was going, she told my sister. We didn't talk for months after that. I eventually forgave her and my mom let me start hanging out with them once she realized they weren't bad influences on me.

I checked my phone to see if Sarah had responded to my last message. Nothing. I was about to message her again when my mom said, "Finally, we're here." I looked up just in time to see a sign.

WELCOME TO-

"Effing-ham?" I asked.

"It's pronounced 'effing-him,'" my mom corrected.

Jo and I smirked at each other.

We turned onto a dirt road when my dad slowed the car down. I glanced up at what looked like giant cotton balls standing in the middle of the road.

"What is that?" I asked, taking out my earbuds.

"It's a flock of sheep, idiot," Jo said, tapping my arm hard with the back of her hand.

"Ow," I muttered, rubbing my arm. I had a small bruise where she had tapped me; my mother's latest drunken rage trophy. She had sworn that she didn't grab me that hard, even though I told her she was hurting me. All because I hadn't put my laundry away.

We watched and waited as the sheep moved out of the way, to the side of the road. There were two older men standing together. The man who was guiding the sheep smiled at my dad and waved. He was wearing a long-sleeved shirt, trousers with suspenders, and a brown flat cap that reminded me of what golfers wear. The other man had a huge white beard and a mustache that curled up on each side. He was wearing a similar hat, although his was black, a sweater vest over a long-sleeved shirt, a bow tie, and matching plaid pants and jacket. He looked

like a very sophisticated gentleman. My dad waved back and drove on.

As we drove past them, I waved also. The man with the bow tie started to raise his hand and then stopped. He just stared at me, as if he had never seen anyone like me before. Like I was a completely different life form. *Rude*, I thought. If this was any indication of how the summer was going to go, or how the people in this town acted, I was preparing to stay indoors and watch as much television as possible. I turned around and looked at the man with the bow tie. His friend had seemed to carry on with their conversation, but he continued to watch me until we were out of sight.

2

We pulled up into a driveway of a house that looked like something out of a children's story. It was brick with dark green vines crawling up the sides. There was a garden in the front filled with a variety of fruits and vegetables. I also noticed a tire swing hanging from a huge weeping willow tree. The tree provided shade over the left side of the house. How adorable, I thought sarcastically in my mind. As the car was stopped, I saw an old lady come out onto the porch and wave at us.

"Please be on your best behavior. That's Aunt Poppy. We'll be staying with her and Uncle Charles. She's a little odd and I don't want you two giving her a hard time. Especially you," my mom said looking at me.

"Whatever," I replied.

"The kids are old enough to know how to act properly. They're not complete apes," added my dad, winking at Jo and me in the mirror.

"Dan, I was talking to you too."

"Best behavior," Dad said. "Got it."

"Margaret! Margaret Jo, is that you? Oh my goodness gracious!" cried the old lady in a sing-song tone.

We all slowly got out of the car as Aunt Poppy made her way over to us. She was technically my great-aunt since she was Mom's aunt. She had short, curly white hair and wore round glasses. Her cheeks were full and pink, and her smile was so big you could almost see every stained tooth in her mouth.

"Hello Aunt Poppy! How are you?" my mom shouted into the woman's face.

"Dear, I'm old, not deaf. I can hear just fine. And I'm doing-" she stopped and looked at Jo and me.

"Jesus, Mary, and Joseph! Are these the twins? Goodness, the last picture your mother sent me was when you two were wee bit ones in nappies together."

Tears suddenly rolled down her face. Jo and I looked at each other in embarrassment. Jo leaned in to shake the woman's hand.

"It's a pleasure to meet you ma'am."

"Ma'am? Gracious, we're all family here. You can most certainly call me Aunt Poppy, or just Poppy. But never ma'am. That makes me feel old!"

Her face grew solemn.

"You're Joanna, aren't you?"

Jo nodded.

"I could tell by the dark hair," she beamed.

"Hello, Dan. You've aged a bit, haven't you?" Aunt Poppy said, turning to my dad.

"Just trying to keep up with you, Poppy."

Aunt Poppy looked at my dad above her glasses before turning towards me.

"You must be Abigail," she said softly. "You look just like your mother when she was your age."

"Uh..." my mom interjected. "I never wore that much dark makeup."

"Actually I prefer Abby," I said before I could stop myself. My mom gave me a stern look.

"Certainly Abby," replied Aunt Poppy. "And don't be silly, Margaret. She has your eyes and your smile."

My mother and I looked awkwardly at each other. I tried imagining my mom as a teenager and just couldn't see her being anyone I'd want to be friends with. I also had a hard time picturing my mom smiling, which she rarely did.

"Well, Dan, if you will get the luggage, I'll show the children and Margaret the rooms. Then we can all have tea and biscuits."

"Of course," muttered my dad.

Aunt Poppy grabbed my hand, then grabbed Jo's hand, and pulled us up to the house. My mom followed close behind. As soon as we walked into the house, I was overwhelmed with smells I had never smelled before. The house looked so delicate, I was afraid to touch anything. I looked in the living room where there were two big armchairs, a couch, and a small coffee table. There was no sign of a TV anywhere. I made my way over to a large cabinet, filled with collectable plates, coins, glass dolls, and-

"Are these magnets?" I asked. Aunt Poppy giggled.

"Oh yes," she said. "I particularly like the animal head ones. Especially the little fox!"

"Where's Uncle Charles?" Mom asked.

"Charles is out playing cards with some friends," sighed Aunt Poppy as she straightened up a doily on the coffee table. I guessed she had made it herself. "He should be back for tea,"

"How is Uncle Charles doing? Is his leg any better or is it still bothering him?" my mom asked.

"Oh, he keeps me on my toes, like always. And his leg is doing okay. Still has to use a cane, although he absolutely loathes it."

We walked up the stairs and stopped at a door to the left.

"Joanna, dear, this will be your room." My sister looked in and came back out nodding. We continued to walk down the hallway.

"On the left down here is the loo and on the right is your room, Abigail."

"Abby," I murmured as I flicked on the light. The room looked as though no one had set foot in it in a long time. There was dust and cobwebs covering the tables, dresser, and lamps. There were even cobwebs lining the walls. I noticed something else about the room. There were no windows. My heart started racing.

"Do you have a grandfather clock?" I demanded.

"Um, no," Aunt Poppy answered. "Why do you ask?"

"Just...wondering," I murmured as I concentrated on the blue dresser with flowers painted all over it.

Aunt Poppy motioned for me to rejoin the group and we continued. We walked back downstairs past the living room, and into the kitchen, while a million thoughts ran through my head. Was that the room I had seen on the plane? It looked the exact same besides the absence of the grandfather clock. But all of the bizarre furniture was the same. Would I be able to sleep there?

"Abigail?"

I realized my mom, dad, sister, and Aunt Poppy were all looking at me.

"Huh?"

"Your aunt was asking you how school was last year," answered my mom.

"Oh. Um, it sucked. Just like every other year."

"Abby!" cried my mom.

"It's quite alright," Aunt Poppy smiled. "Anyhow, upstairs is just your room, Joanna's room, the upstairs bathroom, and the upstairs closet that leads to the attic. You won't be needing anything from up there, and I'm not quite sure the floor of the attic is sturdy enough for anyone to safely be up there. The main floor is the living room, dining room, and kitchen. Downstairs is the room your parents will be staying in, mine and Uncle Charles's room, the downstairs bathroom, and the storage room, where we keep excess food."

She picked up a sugar bowl and took the lid off, revealing little white cubes. I glanced out the window to the front yard. Except, it wasn't their yard I saw. Instead, it was a wooded area, like a forest. I could hear running water and birds chirping. *Yes, the woods,* a voice called out.

"I told Martha, of course I'd share my harvest with her, if she was willing to share her milk and butter with me," Aunt Poppy continued, although I hadn't been listening. I looked back out the window and the front yard was there again. "You know me, I'm always willing to help but-"

"Aunt Poppy, is there a pond or river around here? Like in a wooded area or something?"

My aunt dropped the sugar bowl and it hit the floor with a mild crash. Sugar cubes bounced around on the floor.

"What did you say?" Aunt Poppy asked, turning to me.

Jo quickly bent down to pick up the sugar cubes and bits of broken bowl. At that moment, my mom grabbed my arm and

20

pulled me into the living room. I winced at her gripping where my bruise was.

"What the hell is the matter with you? I tell you to be on your best behavior and not even an hour later you're already acting stupid, asking about a clock and a pond."

"Why is that such a big deal?"

"I told you to be on your best behavior and not to give her a hard time."

"I'm not giving her a hard time!" I raised my voice.

"Why were you asking about a clock, Abby?"

"Uuurgh, in case I wanted to know what time it was!" I blurted.

"Don't sass me."

"I was just asking random questions!"

"And don't lie to me."

"Oh my god. So I'm not allowed to ask people questions now?"

"I don't know what kind of shit you're trying to pull-"

"Is everything alright?"

My mom and I looked to see Aunt Poppy standing in the doorway. Jo and my dad were standing behind her.

"Everything is fine, Aunt Poppy," my mom said.

"Except for the fact that she has to ask me fifty questions about every little thing and then thinks I'm lying when I answer her," I said.

"That's because most of the time you *are* lying!" yelled my mom. I wanted to hit her. Right in the face; in the same exact place she had hit me. I just didn't want to stoop down to her level.

"I think it'd be best if we all just calm down and have some tea," Aunt Poppy said.

"I don't want any tea," I retorted.

"Don't be disrespectful," my mom growled.

I started to walk away and my mom grabbed my arm again; this time much harder.

"Hey!" she snapped.

"OW!" I yelled as I pulled away. Everyone was still staring.

21

"Yeah!" I said, pulling my arm out of my hoodie and raising the sleeve of my t-shirt up. "You see what she does to me? You see why I disrespect her so much? Because I have no respect for a drunk who hits her kid!"

"Abby!" my dad gasped.

Before anyone could respond I ran out the front door, pushing past my mom. I didn't know where I was going and I didn't care where I was going. I ran as fast as I could through a field until I came to a fence. I hopped over to the other side and decided to keep walking. All I could see around me was tall grass and a random group of sheep. After about ten minutes I could see lights ahead. I was walking into a town and starting to realize I was hungry. I walked past shops and pubs until I came to Trotter's, a small bistro that was still open. I walked in and sat down at the first open table I saw and sighed, glad to be giving my feet a rest.

"Hello, can I start you off with something to drink?"

"Yeah I-" I looked up and stopped. Standing before me was by far the cutest boy I had ever seen in my entire life. He looked around my age and was about six feet tall. He had auburn hair and emerald green eyes. Under his work apron, he was wearing a shirt that had an eagle on it and the letters, "ELRFC."

"I-uh-water, please," was all I could say.

The waiter flashed a smile, nodded, and walked off. I looked at my reflection in the window. Disgusted with how I looked, I quickly fixed my hair as best as I could and wiped the sweat off of my face.

"You look fine," said the waiter, coming back. "Besides being a bit windblown."

I turned around and smiled, taking the glass of water.

"I, um. Thanks."

The waiter sat down in the chair opposite of mine. I could feel my cheeks getting hot.

"Do you know what you want to eat yet? The fish and chips are a classic. I wouldn't recommend the shepherd's pie. It's a tad stoggy."

"Huh?" I asked. "What does that mean?"

"Oh," he blushed. "Well, it's heavy. Bogs you down."

"Oh," I smiled, trying not to stare at him too long. "I'll have the fish and chips."

He wrote down my order and then stuck his hand out at me.

"My name is Callum McGreggor. You're not from around here, are you?" he asked, smiling.

"No," I replied, taking his hand to shake. "My name is Abby Mitchell. I'm from The United States."

"I could tell by the accent."

"I didn't know I had an accent. You have a nice accent though. It's Scottish, right?"

"That's right, very good. So, are you from Los Angeles or somewhere cool like that?"

"Ha! No. I'm from plain, boring Hoboken, New Jersey. But it's pretty close to New York."

"You look anything but plain or boring," he said pointing to my pink hair. "What's New York like?"

"Oh, ya know. Hanging out with celebrities and dining at the most expensive restaurants."

When Callum didn't react to that, I laughed.

"Actually, I've only ever been to New York once and it was to see Cats," I continued. "My dad won tickets through a radio station and took us all to see it."

"Cats?" he asked.

"The musical? A bunch of humans dressed in creepy cat costumes singing about being cats? It's pretty self-explanatory. I don't recommend seeing it unless you want to self-induce a coma."

Callum laughed at this also.

"How old are you?" he asked.

"Sixteen. You?"

"Eighteen," he answered.

An older boy, I thought.

"Is there anything to do around here? Or is it all tea and sheep?"

Callum smiled at me again.

"My shift ends in fifteen minutes and then I'll show you how we have fun around here."

I sat there grinning like an idiot, but I didn't care. My first night in England and I was with the hottest guy! I realized how awful I still looked and walked over to the counter.

"Hey, Callum. Are there any cool clothing stores nearby?"

"Um, everything around here is closing. I could ask my sister if she has anything you could borrow for tonight. Oi, Rachel!"

"Would she have anything that would fit my style?" I asked him quietly.

As soon as I asked the question, the answer walked around the corner. A girl wearing knee-high, chunky, black boots, fishnet stockings, a plaid mini skirt, a white shirt, and black suspenders came up to the counter. She was wearing black eyeliner and eyeshadow and had both her septum and left eyebrow pierced.

"This is Abby," Callum said, nodding to me. "She's from the US. She's going with us to The Fox Hole tonight. Do you have anything she could borrow to wear?"

Rachel looked me up and down for a moment and then, smiling condescendingly, said, "Sure. Come with me."

I followed Rachel to the back room and opened what looked like a closet door. Behind the door was a flight of stairs. I stood still.

"The bedrooms are down here," said Rachel. "Don't worry. We're not going to murder you or anythin'."

"You guys live here?" I asked, following her down.

"Just for now, until we can get a place of our own."

The place was very unkempt, but with two teenagers, I didn't expect it to be tidy. There was a weathered couch with clothes piled on it. There was a chipped wooden coffee table with an old pizza box and several soda cans.

"We just moved back from Scotland," Rachel continued. "We were livin' with our grandparents, but they both passed. I know it's a bit of a mess, but everythin' came free with the flat. Basically everythin' except our clothes was left behind by a previous tenant, so most of the stuff isn't in the best condition. But we don't have to pay rent as long as we work upstairs. Callum has been collectin' any tips we make to help us find a house before school starts in the Autumn. Over here is my room."

As we walked into Rachel's room, I felt like I was stepping back into my own bedroom. There were posters covering every inch of the walls, there were piles of clothes everywhere, and there was an instrument in the corner of the room. I half-expected it to be my guitar.

"Checkin' out my ol' drum set, eh?" asked Rachel.

"This is amazing. It looks just like my room. Except I have mostly American bands and an acoustic guitar. Other than that, yeah, this is it."

"Nice. I'm not quite sure what you're looking for but anything should work. Just smell it first to see if it's clean. And no borrowing knickers; those are off limits. I'll be upstairs helping Callum close up the shop."

I started looking around and trying different things on. I decided on a pair of tight distressed black pants and a purple tube top. I wanted to borrow a pair of Rachel's shoes, but she was a size smaller than me.

I walked back through the main room to go upstairs. The bathroom door was cracked open and I could see Callum in the mirror, washing his face. He had taken his shirt off and was humming a song I didn't recognize. I examined every bit of his exposed body. I noticed a tattoo of a lion on his shoulder blade. I also noticed a scar on his chest. He splashed his face to wash the soap off and some of the water landed on his chest. I watched as the droplets ran down his chiseled chest, through the grooves in his abdomen, all the way down to the waistline of his jeans.

"Checkin' out the view, are we?"

I spun around so hard that I knocked over a stack of books that had been piled on a nearby table. Rachel was standing on the stairs with her arms crossed; a devious smile spread across her face. Callum had turned to look at us.

"Sorry, I was just looking for a bathroom," I blushed as I scrambled to pick up the books. "Sorry."

"I'm almost done, then you can have this one," Callum grinned.

"Oh, thanks," I smiled. "Rachel, do you have any makeup I could use?"

"Do I have makeup?" she repeated. "Ha! Go in there and take a look. Use anything you want."

As I opened the bathroom door, Callum squeezed by and placed his hands on my waist. Butterflies invaded my stomach and I rushed into the bathroom. Five minutes and two coats of eyeliner later, I was ready to go. Callum had on a blue and black plaid button-up on and smelled like cologne.

"That outfit looks good on you," said Callum.

"Thanks," I blushed. "You look nice too."

"Ugh, can you please drool over each other later and close the shop up?" asked Rachel. "I'm ready to go have some fun!"

As Callum was turning the lights off to the café, Rachel pulled me off to the side and lowered her voice.

"You have an eye for my brother and he obviously has an eye for you. But you live in the United States and he'll be stayin' here. Do not hurt him. As long as you know that you'll never be anymore than a summer fling, you can have your little tart fun with him."

I didn't respond as Callum nodded us towards the door.

"Okay ladies, shall we then?" he asked.

Callum locked the front door and we went around to the side of the building. There were two matching Yamaha sports bikes. I looked from Callum to Rachel, who was smiling as she got on one before pulling a hot pink helmet over her head. Callum handed me the helmet off his bike and got on.

"Come on," he grinned.

"I don't know," I said, looking around.

"Come on," he repeated; this time a little softer. "It'll be a short ride, and I promise I won't go too fast. It'll be fun. You'll like it."

"Oh gross," Rachel's voice called out before she revved her engine.

I reluctantly got on behind Callum. I gently placed my hand on his upper waist. He pulled my arm and wrapped it around his stomach.

"You might want to hold on a bit tighter," he whispered.

He started his bike and we were on our way to the Fox Hole. On the way, the night air sent a chill through me and I pushed myself into Callum even more. He smelled so good and even though zipping in and out of cars was terrifying, something about being with Callum made me feel safe. In a few minutes, we slowed down to a stop in front of an old brick building. There was a group of people standing outside, smoking cigarettes.

"Welcome to our secret hideout," Callum winked.

We got off the bikes and Rachel took her helmet off.

"Ready to get aled-up?" she asked.

"What?" I asked, taking my own helmet off.

"Drunk," said Callum.

"Oh. Well, I'm only sixteen," I answered.

"Yeah, same here," said Rachel.

Rachel and Callum walked toward the front door. A big man hopped off a stool and crossed his arms in front of us.

"Oi! I have to take a piss!" Rachel said.

"Sorry mate," the man replied, "we're at capacity."

"Oh come on," Callum begged. "We're just trying to give our American friend a good taste of Brit nightlife."

The man looked at me and raised his eyebrows.

"Pretty please?" Rachel stuck her bottom lip out.

The security guard shook his head and said, "Go on in. Callum, take care of her tonight."

"Thanks Tank, ol' boy," Callum grinned as we walked through the door.

The music playing was very loud and the place was very crowded.

"I'm going to go get us drinks," Rachel announced. "What do you want, Abby?"

"Uh, what do you usually get?" I asked Callum.

"I usually just get a whiskey. But I recommend you get something a little lighter. You wouldn't like whiskey."

"I'll have a bottle of water," I said, avoiding eye contact.

"Nice choice," Callum smirked.

"Lame choice," scoffed Rachel.

I looked at Callum, who was smiling and shrugged. Rachel sauntered off, weaving through people with ease.

"What is this place?" I asked.

"Just a hidden spot for young people to hang out at. As long as no one starts any fights, no one really bothers us."

Callum laughed before continuing, "But it's always been like that, even when our parents were kids and came here."

"Not much of a hidden spot then, is it?" I asked, giggling.

Rachel came back with a bottle of water for me, a glass of whiskey for Callum, and a red drink in a glass for herself. Callum was looking out at the dance floor.

"C'mon, let's get out there," he said, pulling on my arm.

"Don't you want to finish your drink first?" I asked.

"It's called multi-taskin'. I can drink and dance at the same time. Right now I really want to dance with you."

"I'll find a table," called Rachel. "Have fun!"

Callum pulled me onto the dance floor. Although neither of us were good dancers, we still had a great time. One of his hands was gripped tight on my waist and one was holding the glass of whiskey raised in the air. A man ran into us, spilling Callum's drink on me.

"Watch where you're goin'!" yelled Callum.

"Piss off!" the man slurred.

"What did you say?" Callum asked loudly.

The man kept walking. Callum's eyes went dark and for a moment, I thought he was going to go after the guy.

"It's okay," I said. "Don't worry about him."

"Are you okay?" he asked me.

"I'm fine."

"You sure?"

I moved in front of Callum, my back against his chest, and wrapped one of his arms around my bare stomach. I leaned back and my lips brushed his ear.

"Never been better," I said.

We started dancing again, this time a bit more intimately. Callum held me tightly as our bodies pushed up against each other. My heart was racing and every time we made eye contact, I thought it was going to explode out of my chest. After a while we stopped to catch our breath and to find Rachel, but didn't see her anywhere.

"She's probably gone to the toilet," Callum said. "Would you like another water?"

I nodded and followed him up to the bar.

"Two waters please," ordered Callum.

The bartender handed him two bottles while Callum placed the money down on the counter. We found an open table and sat down.

"I thought all European boys did was drink alcohol," I said loudly.

"And I thought all American girls were conceited," he said smiling. "I guess we all get proven wrong at some point."

I smiled back at him as he reached his hand across the table and grabbed mine. Although his hands were much bigger than mine, he held my hands ever so gently.

"You're very beautiful. You know that, don't you?"

I looked at him for a moment and found myself leaning forward. Then I realized he was leaning forward also. My lips touched his lips and the whole world seemed to melt away; the whole place seemed to go quiet and still. He cupped my cheek with his hand and I parted my lips to let his tongue in.

"Sorry, am I interrupting?"

Callum and I separated and looked up to see Rachel standing slanted over us holding a drink.

"Bloody hell! First date and already snoggin'? You must really like her, Callum!"

Rachel fell into my lap and put her arms around my neck. I could smell the bitter liquor on her breath that reminded me of my mother.

"So tell me, Abby," Rachel said through more slurred words. "How long before you plan to make the two-backed beast with my brother?"

"What?" I asked.

"He's a virgin, ya know?" she winked. "Wouldn't think so by the looks of him. But he's always been a wee bit shy around the girls."

"I think you've had enough for tonight, Rachel," Callum said, walking over to stand Rachel up. He pulled on her arm and she swatted him away.

"I think you've had enough, *Callum*. What would Selene think of you snogging some girl in a club?"

Callum winced at this last part.

"Selene doesn't have a say in what I do and neither do you!" he yelled.

Callum looked over at me and gently said, "I'm sorry. I'll get a cab to take you home. I just really need to get her out of here before she causes a scene."

I looked into Callum's beautiful green eyes and saw something in them. Embarrassment? Disappointment? Shame? I nodded and we left Rachel slumped over the table. Callum slid his bottle of water into her hand and we headed towards the door. Suddenly, the atmosphere changed. The music seemed too loud and the smell of alcohol and sweat made me nauseous. I had been too naive to think I had met a completely wonderful guy from another country who thought I was wonderful who was single. Of course he had a girlfriend, and I was just some foreign girl he wanted to have fun with for the night. If he would have been upfront about having a girlfriend, that would have been okay. I would at least have had friends to hang out with. Instead, he made me feel foolish.

"I'm sorry for that in there," said Callum, after he called for a taxi. "That wasn't Rachel, that was the alcohol talking. She's been having a hard time...coping with things lately."

"Oh it's fine," I responded quickly. "I just hope what happened between us doesn't affect you and Selene."

Callum looked at me for a moment, thinking of what to say.

"I was afraid to mention Selene because I thought you would think less of me. I respect her for who she is, but she doesn't dictate my life."

A taxi pulled up beside us.

"I have to go," I muttered before getting in.

"Maybe you could stop by the shop again," Callum said, grabbing the door. "I still owe you fish and chips."

"It's fine," I said. "I'm not sure when I'll be back around."

"Won't I see you again?" Callum asked.

I couldn't answer. I grabbed the door and shut it before telling the driver the street I needed. I turned around to watch Callum, still standing on the sidewalk alone. I contemplated what would happen when I arrived back at Aunt Poppy's house. Would my mom dare to lay a hand on me in front of other family members? Or were Aunt Poppy and Uncle Charles also the type of people who thought it was okay to hit their kids?

I checked my phone and saw I had a text message.

Finally, Sarah, I thought. Except it wasn't from Sarah. It was from Jo.

Going to bed. Hope you're okay. I can tell Mom is pissed, so be prepared to have a deadbolt put on your door when you come back. Love you.

3

The taxi stopped at the end of the driveway and I got out after paying. It was a little after one in the morning, so I knew I was in big time trouble. The car pulled away and I stood in the middle of the driveway for a moment, taking in what I thought would be my last bit of freedom for a while. My mom was most likely going to ground me for the whole summer after what I had done.

"Hello," a voice right behind me said.

I turned around and didn't see anyone.

"H-h-hello?" I called out.

I walked out into the middle of the road and saw a in the dark. It looked like a girl, wearing a yellow dress. She seemed to be peering out from behind a large tree on the side of the road.

"Can I help you?" I asked loudly.

She stood still, not saying a word. This was starting to freak me out. The wind picked up and I wrapped my arms around myself. Rustling from behind me made me spin on my heels. It was the breeze blowing a rose bush against the side of the house. I turned to face the girl again and she was gone. Not wanting to be alone out in the dark for another second, I quickly made my way up to the front door and tiptoed inside. I took another step and the floor creaked under my weight.

"Up late, aren't we?"

I made a tiny yelp and turned around quickly to see an old man sitting in an armchair, reading a book. There was a cane on the floor beside him.

"You must be Uncle Charles," I sighed, grabbing my chest.

"And you must be Abigail."

"Abby, actually."

"Yes, of course. I heard about your little tiff you got into with your mother earlier. Everyone's been quite worried about you, you know."

"Everyone except my mom," I replied, sitting in the chair next to Uncle Charles. I suddenly realized how exhausted I was.

"Especially your mother," he replied, not looking up from his book. "Why did you run away?"

"Why does your house smell so funny?" I asked. It was rude, I know. But I was desperately trying to evade the subject.

"I asked you first."

I sat there a moment, debating how to answer him.

"My mom doesn't understand me. She doesn't even try to. And she doesn't respect or trust me, for that matter."

Uncle Charles made an "mmm" sound that said go on.

"And, I don't know. Sure I've lied to her before, but she acts like everything I say is a lie. If she's not going to trust me or believe me, why bother telling the truth."

I waited for him to say something. He closed his book and sat it on the coffee table in front of us.

"A person can lie once and be accused of being a liar once. But, if that person keeps on lying, then they are a liar."

I frowned.

"They become unknown to their family; a total stranger. How could your mom understand you if you don't allow her to get to know you?"

And here I was, half-expecting this old man to be on my side. Of course not. He picked up his cane and stood up, yawning.

"Well, night then."

"Wait!" I said, crossing my arms. "You never answered my question. Why does-"

"I remember the question. Why does my house smell odd? Part of it is from my tobacco pipe, part of it is from Poppy's lavender perfume, and part of it is because we keep bergamot oil around the house to remind us of our daughter. It was her favorite scent."

"You have a daughter?" I asked. Mom had never mentioned having a cousin.

"We did have one. She died some time ago."

Uncle Charles was standing there smiling sadly at me. I wanted to say something but didn't quite know what. He turned to go upstairs.

"Good night Uncle Charles. It was nice meeting you."

"It was nice meeting you too, finally."

I watched as Uncle Charles hobbled down the hallway and out of sight. I turned off of the downstairs light and went up to my room. I stared at the bed, remembering the weird, wobbly one from the vision I had on the plane. I reached down and gave it a push. Just a regular mattress. I laughed in relief before realizing how creepy the dark room suddenly seemed, as if someone were watching me. I was too tired, and quite frankly, too scared, to unpack my pajamas, so I got into bed with my clothes still on. It made me realize that I was still wearing Rachel's clothes. I would have to return them to her eventually and get mine back. I closed my eyes and fell asleep instantly.

I could hear rushing water, like a faucet. Was it morning already? My eyes fluttered open and I looked around. I was in the woods, sitting leaned up against a tree. There was a book beside my knees, in the fallen leaves. I must have fallen asleep while reading. The Notebook was my favorite, and no matter how many times I read it, it still made me cry. The story of Noah and Allie's love made me long for something similar. This copy of the book was also my favorite because it had a handwritten note from my best friend on the inside cover. I stretched and scratched until I was comfortably awake.

I stood up slowly and looked down at my stomach. I couldn't wait until she came back. It had been so long since I last saw her. And a lot sure had changed, that much was certain. I walked through the forest, running my hand along the moss on a tree trunk, pausing to listen to the birdsong, and picking some things here and there for Mother. Mother especially needed more mugwort and dandelions. I stopped suddenly when I noticed a perfect ring of mushrooms. A fairy circle! I had never seen one before but Mother had told me about them. I couldn't wait to tell her I had found one. Maybe she would want to join me later to dance around the outside of it. It was a full moon, after all. I bit my lip, thinking of the lore. If you stepped into a fairy circle, it meant you would certainly die at a young age.

I sat up in bed, jolting awake. I could smell food and heard clanging from the kitchen downstairs. I had a headache and I was uncomfortable from sleeping in clothes that weren't pajamas. I got up, changed my clothes, put my hair up in a messy bun, and used some makeup remover wipes to take off any evidence of the previous night. I went downstairs and the first person I saw was my dad. He was sitting on the sofa, reading a newspaper and drinking tea. He looked up at me and put the cup and paper down so abruptly that tea splashed onto the paper.

"Abby!" He got up and hugged me. "Oh, Abby, you're safe. I was so worried about you! Where were you? Are you okay?"

"I'm fine Dad, really. I was with some really nice people last night. I stayed out of trouble. Promise."

Then, my mom and Aunt Poppy walked into the room. My mom looked like she had gotten as much sleep as I had, maybe less.

"Oh gracious!" Aunt Poppy moved my dad out of the way to hug me. "You had us very worried, young lady!"

"Sorry," I blushed.

"I'll go get you some tea and after you finish, go up and take a nice, hot bath."

She hurried back into the kitchen, leaving my mom and I to stare at each other.

"Mom, I'm really-"

"Don't worry about it."

"But Mom, I'm trying to apologize here," I stepped closer to her.

"I figured you would come back," muttered my mom. "I was just giving you the space you needed."

"Thanks," I said. "Listen, I promise I stayed out of trouble. I didn't do anything I wasn't supposed to."

35

She raised her eyebrows at me.

"Well, besides running off and staying out late."

She didn't respond.

"And I fully accept any consequences that are coming my way," I added. "So if you want to ground me or take my phone away-"

"You're fine," said my mom quietly.

"What?" I asked, surprised. "You're not mad at all?"

"Well I'm not happy about what happened but I figure I can't control what you do. So, why waste my breath telling you no?"

Aunt Poppy cleared her throat loudly from the other room.

"Meaning..." my mom continued, "I need to trust you more to make the right choices. And in return I expect more honesty and respect."

For the first time in years, I wanted to hug my mom. We stood there awkwardly, neither of us knowing what else to say. She wasn't giving me any signs that she wanted a hug, so I let the moment pass. Instead, I gave her a half smile and walked into the kitchen to get something to eat.

"Here's your tea, dear," said Aunt Poppy softly, handing me a cup. "Listen, Abby, about what happened between your mother and you yesterday- well, it's none of my business of course- I just want to tell you that your mother has had a very challenging life-"

"Haven't we all?" I asked, but Aunt Poppy continued.

"-And I just ask that you take it easy on her. At least just for the time that you're here."

"You want me to take it easy on *her*?" I asked, my temper rising. "Look, I don't know what my mom has been through, nor do I really care. It's no excuse for her to treat me and Jo, more me, like she does. She's hurt me before. She's even slapped me."

Aunt Poppy blinked several times at me in shock.

"She has a drinking problem," I added. "She doesn't think so but she drinks like, half a bottle of wine *every night*. Like she can't cope without it."

Aunt Poppy put her hand up to her mouth and sighed.

"I'm sorry, dear. If you ever want to talk about it, I am always here for you. I'll try and see what I can do to help her. I just don't want you running off until all hours of the night. Not while you're here in my house."

I looked at her. She raised her eyebrows at me.

"Do we have a deal?" she asked.

I didn't move.

"I said, do we have a deal?" she repeated.

I nodded.

"Good!" she said cheerfully.

"Do you have anything to eat?" I asked, wanting the subject to change.

"Of course! I made some blueberry muffins and there are apples on the counter."

I took one sip of my tea, almost gagged, and dumped it into the sink as soon as Aunt Poppy walked into the other room. I grabbed an apple and went back upstairs to unpack. When I walked into my room, my dad was standing over empty suitcases holding my teddy bear I had packed.

"Your mom and I got this for you for your first birthday. I didn't know you still even liked it."

"Yeah, I don't know how that got in there," I said, grabbing the bear and tossing it onto my bed. I smirked at my dad as he smiled at me.

"I didn't unpack your- uh- personal items because I thought you'd be embarrassed if I saw them."

"You mean *you'd* be embarrassed," I laughed.

"Well, that too."

I grabbed an outfit that my dad had already unpacked, then grabbed a pair of underwear and a bra from my suitcase.

"Hey, at least I wear underwear," I laughed. "It could be worse."

"Ha, ha, very funny. Are you taking a bath right now?"

"Yeah, I suppose so. Why?"

"I'll have to help you."

"Help me?" I asked. "I'm a little too old to have someone help me take a bath."

"Not that kind of help. Just come on. You'll see what I mean."

I followed my dad into the bathroom and watched him turn the faucet. There was a loud popping sound, followed by a long, whining moan. Soon, yellowish water started spurting out of the faucet.

"Ugh!" I gasped. "What's wrong with their water?"

"Give it a moment."

I watched as the water turned clear and my dad smiled at me.

"Their pipes are old and starting to rust. When water sits in the pipes overnight, it turns the water a funky color. You just need to let it run until it becomes clear."

"And we've been drinking that water," I groaned.

"They have filtered water through their fridge, Abby. It's an old house."

"It's a creepy house," I corrected. "My room doesn't even have windows in it."

"It was Uncle Charles' childhood home. The room you're in and the one Jo's in used to be one room. It was the primary bedroom, but they renovated it to make it two, smaller rooms. Which is why Jo's room has windows and yours doesn't. Then, they added on to the main floor to make their room and another room to be used as an office or spare bedroom. But the house is still old and probably could benefit from new plumbing."

My dad ran his hand under the water.

"How's that?" he asked.

"I would have preferred it to be warmer but beggars can't be choosers I suppose," I answered, checking the water's temperature.

"Well, it'll help you get done quicker," Dad winked.

He left the bathroom and shut the door. I let my hair down and shook it, realizing for the first time that I smelled bad, like a combination of stale beer and cigarettes. When the tub was full enough, I turned off the faucet. I added the bath oil to the tub. It smelled very strongly of orange, but a little spicy. I stepped into the tub and sat down very carefully so I wouldn't slip and fall. The smell filled my nostrils and I was reminded of something happy, like Christmas.

I closed my eyes and breathed in the citrus scent, thinking of Callum. I wondered what he was doing. Was he thinking about me? Was he with Selene? Did he think Selene was prettier than me? Was Rachel concerned about getting her clothes back? Suddenly, the water in the tub started vibrating and the bathroom seemed to be falling away from me.

I was in the forest. I had only my nightgown on since I hadn't bothered to get dressed. Sneaking out of the house had been enough of a challenge without spending the extra time to change clothes. I knew I should have at least grabbed a pair of shoes, but being barefoot never really bothered me. The cold ground was hard and the night air was brisk. But this was my only chance to dance around the fairy ring. It was the last night of the full moon and if I wanted luck and good fortune, I would need to dance around the circle nine times. I was almost running to the place with excitement. Mum had not wanted to join me. She had been cross with me recently. Well, she had been cross with me for the past nine months.

The clouds were covering the moon, making the forest darker than usual. I had not wanted to bring my flashlight so I wouldn't disturb the creatures of the woods. My Gran had moved here from Ireland with my mother and her sister when she no longer felt safe. She was a pagan, who honored flora and fauna, and worshiped many deities of nature. In simple terms; a witch. Growing up around Gran, I learned a lot, just as my mother had when she was young. I learned about the Triple Goddess, remedies, charms, rituals, and even curses; although Mum forbade me to use any curses. My aunt had moved to the United States at a young age, eventually getting married, and having a little girl of her own. But over time, my aunt subdued her special gifts that the women in our family possess, made us all swear not to tell or teach my cousin.

 Ever since we were little girls, we knew we were special. She was two years older than me, but I had developed my gifts first. Every summer, we would spend most of our days outside, playing and learning the ways of nature. She was always impressed by my knowledge of trees and flowers. I knew all of the birds by their calls and could name most insects we came across. One time we saw an adder, the only venomous snake in the region, and we watched as it wriggled around on the ground, shedding its skin. I remembered my grandma saying that snakes embodied psychic energy, and that snakes shedding their skin was a sign of a new beginning. That following week, Gran passed away peacefully in her sleep. The night she died, I saw her in my dreams. She told me that she had died and not to be sad. When I talked to my cousin about it, she shockingly told me that she had had the exact same dream.

 I reached the fairy ring and was relieved to see it still intact. As I got closer, the clouds moved to reveal the huge full moon. I gave my thanks to the moon for providing light before picking up the bottom of my nightgown and dancing around the circle. I went around once, then twice. I thought of all of the love and happiness in my life. I went around a third and fourth time, looking forward to the future. I danced a fifth and sixth circle, praying for protection and serenity. I completed my seventh and eighth circles, invoking the elements as I did so. As I was dancing around the ninth time, I honored my ancestors and asked that they bless me.

 Just before I completed the ninth circle, I heard a twig snap nearby. The sudden sound in the quiet forest startled me. I dropped the end of my nightgown and spun around, tripping over the fabric. I stumbled onto the wet grass, landing on my hip. I was quick enough to brace my stomach as I landed. I froze for a moment, catching my breath and waiting to see what had made the noise. Then I realized where I had landed; right into the inside of the fairy ring. I swiftly stood up and suddenly felt very afraid.

"Hello?" I called out, wiping the mud off my palms. When I saw a large shadow move through the trees, I ran as fast as I could. I knew there was always a possibility of bears, especially in the woods. I didn't stop running until I saw my street. Once I reached my driveway, I turned towards the woods. I could barely make out a figure along the treeline. Not a bear. A man. A very large man. And he was watching me.

I came back and splashed water onto the bathroom floor, gasping hard. The sound of feet thudded up the stairs and my dad's voice called, "Is everything okay in there?"

"Uh, yeah," I said, shaking. "Thought I saw a huge spider. Sorry."

It had been like a dream, but hadn't at the same time, just like what had happened on the airplane. I knew I had been sitting in the bathtub the whole time but it was like I had gone to the woods, smelling the moss, hearing the birds, feeling my hip hit the ground. I looked down at my shaking hands and saw nothing but drops of water falling from my wet hair.

All at once the lights in the bathroom started flickering and the cabinets opened, then slammed shut, and then opened again. All of a sudden, the water in the tub grew uncomfortably hot. I jumped out of the tub and threw a towel around me. The water in the tub started boiling. I reached for the door and turned the knob but it wouldn't open.

"Help! Someone! I can't get the door open!"

The lights went out and I looked down at my arm as a decayed hand gripped it.

"Help me," a voice whispered in my ear.

I closed my eyes and screamed. The door opened, sending me backwards onto the floor.

"What's wrong!" asked my dad.

"The lights!" I cried.

"What about the lights, honey?"

41

I opened my eyes. The bathroom was lit like normal and the cabinets were closed.

"The water in the tub was scalding and the cabinet doors were opening and closing on their own."

My dad gave me a funny look.

"Sweetie, I'm sure the light bulb is just old and getting ready to go out."

"And the cabinets?" I asked.

"Well, maybe your mind is just playing tricks on you."

"Right," I retorted. "That must be it. You can leave now."

Mad at him for not believing me, I shut the door in my dad's face and put my clean clothes on and combed my hair. I went down the stairs ten minutes later, sketch book in hand, and was about to open the door.

"Where are you going?" asked Jo.

"Don't worry about it," I replied, smiling.

"Well there's no way you've already made a friend here."

"I made two, actually. See, unlike you, I'm willing to get out and have some fun."

"Is that what they're calling STDs now?"

"You're disgusting," I scoffed.

"What are your friends' names?" Jo laughed.

"Callum and Rachel."

"Boyfriend and girlfriend?"

"Brother and sister. Why?"

"Oh," she muttered. "Mom wanted us to clean and dust our rooms."

"I'll do it later!" I retaliated, shutting the door behind me.

Now, in the daylight, I could see a big tree where the girl had been the night before. I started to make my way towards it when I heard my mom call out, "Tomorrow you're spending the whole day with the family, no exceptions!"

"Whatever, fine!" I yelled back.

I passed the big tree and stood at the edge of the woods. I turned to see Aunt Poppy's house, which looked so small, like a doll house. A few minutes later, the trees were so thick, I couldn't see the house anymore. I walked a bit further and stopped to hear the sound of rushing water. Following the sound, I eventually came to a stream, the water gently trickling through the various rocks and sticks. It was as good a place as any to relax and sketch. I climbed up onto a particularly large rock that was raised higher on one side, giving it an almost chair-like shape. I closed my eyes and leaned back on it. I felt something with my fingertips. I looked down to see a carving in the stone;

O & M

I ran my fingers over the letters and I pictured who must have done it.

Two blonde little girls were in the creek, splashing in their swimsuits. One of the little girls, the one with shorter hair, took a small, sharp rock and brought it over to the boulder I was sitting on. I watched her carve the letters as the other girl, the one with the long braid, ran over.

"Don't do that!" she cried.

"I'm just putting our initials. No one else will see it."

"It doesn't matter! You shouldn't do that. It's vandalism. Marking or carving stones isn't okay."

"It's just a rock!"

"It's part of nature! Part of Earth. You must treat it kindly."

"I'm sorry."

She dropped the sharp rock onto the mossy ground and hung her head. The girl with the braid grabbed her hand and smiled. They ran back to the water, giggling and splashing. And then they disappeared completely.

When I looked around, it was just me in the woods.

"Vivid imagination," I laughed to myself.

I opened my sketch book and thought about what I wanted to draw. I looked around for some inspiration and then thought about the fairy ring I had seen while taking a bath. I put the pencil against the paper and began drawing the scene. The ghostly-looking woman in her white gown, dancing around the circle of mushrooms under a full moon. Something about her seemed so familiar to me, although I had no idea what her face looked like. I had *been* her in my vision, so I left any details of her out of the drawing. Instead, I drew her from behind, showing her long, wavy hair swaying with her movement.

"What're you drawing?"

4

I shrieked at the voice cutting through the silence. I looked down and saw a girl who looked about my age, maybe a bit older. She was petite with long blonde hair in a ponytail and was wearing a yellow dress.

"Can I help you?" I asked sternly. "You scared the crap out of me!"

"I'm sorry," she smiled. "I thought you heard me approaching."

I didn't respond.

"So?" she nodded towards my journal.

"Oh, um, it's not that good," I said, handing it to her. "And it's not quite finished."

She looked at the drawing I had been working on. Her eyes widened and then met mine.

"You drew this?" she asked. I nodded.

She flipped through the pages of my sketch book.

"Oh," I blushed. "Those are..."

"These are fantastic!" she gasped. "You're so talented!"

"Thanks."

"Did you just move here?" she asked.

"Um, no. I'm staying at my aunt's house," I replied, pointing my finger in the direction of the house.

"Who's your aunt? Maybe I know her."

"Poppy," I said through gritted teeth.

"You must be her great niece. She's much too old to have a niece your age."

"No, that would be my mom."

The two of us stood there waiting for the other to say the next thing. I was hoping she would say goodbye but instead she just stood there smiling. I finally broke the silence.

"Well it was nice meeting you-uh-"

"My name is Olivia," she flipped her long ponytail back. "What's yours?"

"I'm Abby."

"Abby. That's a very pretty name, Abby. How old are you?"

"Sixteen. You?"

"I'm eighteen. Wow, sixteen years old. Seems like yesterday."

"It was only two years ago. You sound like an old person."

"Would you want to, I don't know...hang out over the summer? Just to have someone to talk to. A friend."

"Okay," I said. "Sure, I'll hang out with you."

The smile started to reappear on Olivia's face.

"So, do you like it here in England so far?"

"It's okay, I guess," I said, picking up a stick and throwing it into the water. Olivia didn't say anything. "I mean, I've only been here for a day. And I thought we'd be staying closer to the city than out in the country. Not to mention the house I'm staying in is dirty and smells weird. I figured my aunt and uncle would be strict since they're from the same family as my mom. But they're pretty cool for old people."

Olivia still didn't say anything.

"Uh, but I did meet two pretty cool people last night. A brother and sister from Scotland. We went to this secret hangout spot and it was really fun. But then I found out the hot brother who was flirting with me had a girlfriend and the sister got mad at me for kissing him so I came home."

I stopped and looked at Olivia, who had her head resting on her hands, smiling.

"I'm not boring you, am I?" I asked.

"Not at all. I think it's fascinating listening to you. It's not every day I... come across a girl close to my age around here. Especially one from America."

I smiled vaguely at her and then looked back at the creek.

"We used to go to a place called The Fox Hole," Olivia giggled. "That was the spot for kids to hang out at."

"That's where we went," I smiled.

46

"Wow, it's still there?" she asked.

"Huh?"

"Want to go for a swim?" asked Olivia, ignoring me.

"No. I mean, I don't even have a swimsuit."

Olivia straightened up and brushed off her dress.

"Come on," she smiled. "I want to show you something."

Reluctantly, I slid off the boulder and followed her. We started walking along the creek for a while. Olivia was kind of a strange girl, but something drew me to her. I felt like I somehow knew her already.

"Those are elderberries right there," Olivia pointed to a shrub with dark berries on it. "Very good for the immune system."

She skipped over to a group of small white flowers.

"And this is yarrow! So many benefits! Mending wounds, menstrual pain, anxiety and depression relief, and digestive health."

She picked a small bundle and gently tucked it behind my ear.

"Truly magical," she smiled at me.

Oh god, I thought. *Does she think there's chemistry here or what?*

Suddenly, Olivia stopped smiling. Her eyes widened.

"What is it?" I asked.

"Shh! Come here, quick!" she whispered, grabbing my hand.

We crept behind a large, fallen tree trunk. Olivia and I peeked over the top to watch as a man who appeared to be in his early thirties, walked by up ahead. He had to be over six feet, weighing at least 250 pounds. He looked like a professional wrestler with bulging bicep muscles stretching the sleeves of his shirt. The man had black hair with a thin line of white on one side and a dark, chiseled face. He stopped by the water and pulled something shiny out of his pocket.

The sun hit the object and caused a beam to shine right into my eyes. I squinted hard, trying to watch the man. It must have been the sun bouncing off the water, but the outline of the man seemed blurry. He kissed the object and suddenly dropped it into the stream. Then the man walked off and disappeared into the woods.

"Who the hell was that?" I asked Olivia after she sighed and clutched her chest.

"Mr. Harvey," she murmured. "Seamus Harvey."

"What's that matter?" I noticed tears filling her eyes.

"He's...not a good person. He's a very evil man. He...does bad things to people. To girls."

Olivia was holding herself, not looking at me. I suddenly realized what Olivia was insinuating. Had this Harvey man done something bad to her? Had she seen him do something bad to someone else?

"Have you told anyone?" I asked her, swallowing the lump in my throat. "Have you at least told your parents?"

"I've tried."

"And?"

"They wouldn't listen."

"Olivia-"

"I need to go," said Olivia, quickly standing and wiping her cheeks. "I'm sorry. Will you be able to come back tomorrow?"

"I can't," I said. "I have to spend the day with my family. I'm so sorry."

"Okay. Well, this is pretty much all I do all day every day so whenever you want to hang out, I'll be here. And maybe you could bring your sister sometime."

Had I mentioned Jo?

I nodded and said goodbye. As I made my way back to the house, it began to rain; softly at first, but as I reached the street, it started pouring. I ran the rest of the way, my heart pounding in my chest. I hoped Olivia had gotten home before it started raining. Thinking about what she said, seeing her face when we saw that man, made me sick to my stomach. I got inside the house and kicked my wet shoes off, shivering. The stinging mixture of smells hit my nose and I flopped down into the chair next to Uncle Charles.

"Looks to be a promising day," he said, not looking up from his book.

"Yeah," I muttered.

"What have you been up to?"

"Oh, wandering around. Trying to just pass the time."

"I hear ya," sighed Uncle Charles.

I studied him while he read his book. His head seemed almost too small for his body and was almost completely bald. His reading glasses sat at the tip of a round, large nose and were magnifying two bright blue eyes. As he read, he made a clicking sound and shook his head.

"What's wrong?" I asked.

"Just realized, the weatherman predicted sunny with a high of 85. Imagine, getting paid just to stand there and guess."

I started laughing and saw a glimpse of a smile right before he straightened up and continued reading.

"Abigail, I'm so glad you're home," cried Aunt Poppy coming in from the kitchen. "I saw some robins hiding under a bush this morning, so I figured that meant rain was on the way."

Uncle Charles sighed and shook his head, turning the page of his book loudly.

"Your mother is cleaning the room she and your father are staying in. Go and see if she needs your help."

"Do I have to?" I asked.

She looked at me above her glasses. I obeyed Aunt Poppy and went to look for my mom.

"Mom?" I called out.

"Yeah?" I heard her say.

I followed her voice and walked into her room to find my mom scrubbing away at the floor.

"I wish Aunt Poppy had a mop. Will you message your dad and ask him to pick one up while he's out?"

"Do you want some help?" I asked while I pulled my phone out.

She stopped and looked up at me.

"You're kidding me, right?"

49

"Look," I said, "if you don't want my help just say so. I'm offering though. Rare opportunity."

She sat up a moment, stretching her back.

"Um sure. Grab a rag and wipe off that mirror over there."

I did as she said and started wiping away at the caked-on dust. Neither of us talked while we worked. Occasionally, my mom would start humming a song, but whenever she caught me watching her, she'd immediately stop.

For the next couple of hours, my mom and I went through different parts of the house dusting, washing, and vacuuming. Jo somehow got out of helping us and went with Uncle Charles to go play cards with an old friend. Meanwhile, Aunt Poppy went out to shop for dinner.

"Why does she let the house get like this?" I asked after scrubbing the lime off the upstairs bathroom faucet.

"She cleans the parts of the house that she uses. They're both older now, so it's getting harder to maintain the house."

I looked down at my mom as she cleaned the tub. She looked pretty even though she was sweaty and covered in dust and grime. She had her hair back and a bandana covering the ponytail.

"What I wouldn't do for a stand up shower right now," she said.

"Yeah, no kidding. I feel like I'm going to bathe less just because it's a pain to deal with every time." I winked.

"Just make sure you don't stink up the place," my mom laughed.

"I won't."

"Not like anyone would be able to tell in this house," she added. "Between the lavender, tobacco, and orange-"

"Bergamont," I corrected.

"Bergamont," she smiled. "How did you know?"

"Uncle Charles told me," I chuckled, "when I came home that first night."

My mom grew serious.

"Abby, can I ask you something?"

50

"Sure," I nodded.

"What exactly happened the first night?"

I sighed, thought about what I was going to say, and told my mom what had happened that night with Rachel and Callum, leaving out only the part about kissing Callum.

"You didn't drink at all?" she asked.

"No," I answered. "I only had water. I swear."

"Good," her voice cracked. "I'm glad to hear you're not turning out like me."

"Mom-"

But before I could get another word out, she took the curtains and rug out of the room. I finished the sink and tub while I waited for her to come back. After she still didn't come back, I decided to wash my hands and chill in my room. I sketched in my journal until I heard everyone return from their outings. When I went downstairs, I saw that Uncle Charles had fallen asleep in his chair. Aunt Poppy and Jo were in the kitchen talking and working on dinner. My dad was sitting on the couch, doing a crossword puzzle and drinking tea.

"How can you drink that?" I whispered, sitting down next to him.

"You get used to it after the first fifty your aunt offers you."

He went back to his puzzle.

"You doing okay, kiddo?" he asked me.

"Yeah, I guess. I don't know what's gotten into me. I'm having these...strange things happening to me. I'm making an effort to be nicer to Mom. Maybe I do need to start drinking the tea here."

Dad laughed at this remark and then scowled at the puzzle.

"I'll never finish that stupid thing," he said pointing at it.

I picked up the puzzle and started looking at the clues.

"Number two down is eggs... number eleven down is vampire...number twenty-one across is disco."

I looked over at my dad, who was frowning.

"Let me see that."

He studied the puzzle, got out his pencil again, and started filling them in.

"Well I'll be goddamned."

"DAN!" yelled Aunt Poppy. Uncle Charles jolted awake. "I will not have that kind of language in my house!"

"Sorry, Poppy," apologized my dad, blushing.

"It's quite alright. Just don't let it happen again. You're never too old to have your mouth washed out with soap."

She popped her head into the room and turned to me, smiling.

"Dinner will be ready soon, so go freshen up."

"I don't need to freshen anything up."

"She means go wash your hands," whispered Uncle Charles.

"Oh."

While I was washing my hands, I realized how hungry I was. I had not eaten much in the last two days and I was ready to just unhinge my jaws and tilt my head back while my dad poured food down my throat. I ran downstairs and smelled a wonderful odor that almost overpowered the tobacco-bergamot-lavender stench of the house. I sat down at the table and looked to see what Aunt Poppy was bringing out. She sat the platter down and I scowled.

"What's the matter, dear?" asked Aunt Poppy.

"What is that," I asked quietly.

"We had this at scout camp one year," Dad said casually. "It's pretty good but it has a better taste if you catch it yourself."

"Oh I know what you mean," said Uncle Charles. "I miss getting out to hunt."

"Can someone please tell me what this is?" I asked. "Or at least what it once was?"

"It's roast duck, Abigail," answered my aunt.

"I'm not hungry anymore," I muttered, disgusted.

"Oh come on, Abby," said my sister. "It's like chicken."

"Funny how everyone always seems to use that for things that aren't like chicken at all!"

"It's more gamey than chicken," Uncle Charles explained.

"Gamey?" I repeated.

"Dear, you haven't hardly eaten anything since you've arrived," said Aunt Poppy, taking my plate and plopping glazed carrots onto it. "I hope you're not trying to be like those runway models I see on the front of the magazines. Showing off everything God gave them, with their ribs sticking out and everything."

"Poppy," grunted Uncle Charles.

"I'm just saying!" she said.

"Please just try it," my dad begged.

I looked around at my dad, Jo, Uncle Charles, Aunt Poppy, and finally my mom.

"What do you think?" I asked her.

"Do whatever you want," she said in a low voice.

"I mean, what do you think of the duck?"

"Do you honestly care what I think?" she asked.

"I'm asking you, aren't I?"

"It tastes like turkey more than chicken. I think you'd like it."

I slowly picked up the carving knife, sliced off a piece of meat, and put it on my plate. After cutting off a small bite and placing it in my mouth, I chewed slowly, as if waiting for it to explode.

"It's not bad," I said finally.

"There you go!" cried Aunt Poppy, carving another slice of meat for me. "You never know unless you try it first!"

"Next, we'll have you try good ol' English fish and chips," Uncle Charles laughed. "We'll make you a proper Brit by the end of summer!"

The mention of fish and chips made me think of Callum. A part of me wished I would have gotten his or Rachel's number. He had a girlfriend, but maybe we could try being friends. Aunt Poppy had made sticky toffee pudding for dessert. It was incredible. I couldn't believe I had never had it before. After dessert, everyone sat in the living room. My dad, Jo, and I sat on the couch, Aunt Poppy and Uncle Charles took the two armchairs, and my mom brought in a chair from the dining room.

We took turns telling stories; how Uncle Charles and Aunt Poppy met, what it was like for Aunt Poppy to grow up in Ireland, when Jo broke her arm attempting to skateboard, and when I played at a coffee shop open mic last spring.

"I can't believe I'm related to a musician!" exclaimed Aunt Poppy.

"Well, I'm not exactly on tour just yet," I laughed.

"Margaret, remember when you and Liv sang Christmas songs for the mayor one year?" Aunt Poppy asked my mom. "You two stood up in front of the busy town square and started singing your hearts out."

Mom looked at Aunt Poppy as if she had just slapped her.

"Oh, you two were so darling!" continued Aunt Poppy, tears building in her eyes. "The mayor said that it was the cutest thing he'd ever seen."

"Why'd ya have to bring her up, Poppy?" asked Uncle Charles harshly. It was the first time I had heard him get angry.

"So are we all supposed to never talk about her again? Just forget about her?" cried Aunt Poppy.

"No, but you know how much it upsets Margaret."

I looked over at my mom. Tears were streaming down her face.

"Mom?" Jo said softly.

Mom quickly stood up and went to her room, leaving the rest of us to sit there in awkward silence. Aunt Poppy slowly stood up, smiled at Jo and me, and went after my mom. My dad went upstairs shortly after Aunt Poppy left the room and didn't come back down.

"Well, looks like I'm bunking with Dad tonight," Jo sighed as she got up. "Goodnight, Abby. Goodnight, Uncle Charles."

"Goodnight," we replied.

I sat there, debating if I should go to my room as well. I didn't know if Uncle Charles wanted me to stick around.

"Guess it's just you and me now, kid," he said. "Unless of course you're leaving me too."

"No, I'll stay awake a bit longer," I smiled.

Uncle Charles reached into his pocket and pulled out his wallet. He started digging through it, obviously trying to find something. He grunted and sighed as he flipped through everything.

"Aha! Here it is," he said, before reaching over to hand me something.

It was a picture of a family; father, a mother, and a little girl. The father was lifting the little girl in the air while the mother was tickling her. The smiles on their faces were so big and bright, even though the picture was faded. The corners were bent from years of being pulled out of the wallet.

"Is this you and Aunt Poppy?" I asked him, although I knew the answer. They looked the exact same, except younger. Uncle Charles nodded and smiled. I pointed at the little girl.

"Is this your daughter?"

He nodded again.

"You would have loved her," he said. "You remind me a lot of her."

"May I...ask how she died?" I handed him back the picture. After putting it back into his wallet, Uncle Charles adjusted himself in his chair to face me.

"Well, the thing is, Abby. We don't know for sure that she *did* die. I think she did, but Poppy believes that our daughter just ran away. It was so long ago though, and with technology today, I think she would have come home by now. I honestly don't think she would have run away in the first place. Despite everything she was going through at the time."

Uncle Charles wiped away his tears.

"The police couldn't find anything that led to Olivia's whereabouts. No body, no witnesses, no leads. Nothing. Just vanished."

"Wait, did you say Olivia?" I asked him.

"Yes. Her name was Olivia."

Holy shit, I thought. The little girl in the photo had long wavy hair, just like the Olivia I had met in the forest. But the little girl had been maybe three years old, and forest Olivia was eighteen. They couldn't have been the same person, could they? Unless she was very young when she went missing. I thought about how I would tell Uncle Charles about her. If they weren't the same person, it might cause a lot of drama with my family. I couldn't possibly give him false hope about his missing daughter. And my mom would never forgive me if I opened old wounds for everyone. I would have to be very careful about how I did this.

"Uncle Charles, I have something to tell you," I said, curling my legs up underneath my bottom. He listened closely.

"Do you know a Mr. Harvey?"

"Seamus Harvey?" asked Uncle Charles. I nodded.

"Yes," he said slowly. "I recall that name quite clearly."

"Did you know he might have...done things to young girls?"

His eyes widened.

"Where on earth did you hear that?" he asked. "And how do you know that name?"

"I saw him in the woods."

"It couldn't have been him."

"Why not?" I frowned.

"Because the only Seamus Harvey I know of died a long time ago. Shortly after Olivia went missing. He was known as being a bit of an oddball. He was a suspect in a missing persons case a couple of years before Olivia went missing. They never found anything to connect him though. And then Olivia's, like the others, went cold. But no, that wasn't who you saw."

"Well maybe it was his son," I said, trying to make sense of what happened in the woods. "Like, Seamus Harvey Jr. or something. One of my new friends identified him."

Uncle Charles shook his head.

"No, he had children, but I don't think either of them were named after him. Your friend was mistaken."

Aunt Poppy had walked back into the room, red-eyed and sniffling.

"She won't talk to me," she murmured.

"I'll try and talk to her," I found myself saying.

I walked down the hall and stood in front of the closed door that led to my mom's room. I wasn't sure what I was going to say to her. Knocking first, I opened the door. My mom was curled up in the bed, facing away from the door. I walked towards the bed, not sure if she was awake.

"I told you, I don't want any tea. I just want to be left-"

"Mom?" I interrupted her.

She sat up and turned around. Her face was puffy and red from the crying.

"What are you doing?" she asked coldly.

I sat down on the bed beside her and slowly put my arms around her. At first she was tense, and then she slowly lowered her guard and let me hug her. I had never comforted my mom before. I felt her shoulders bounce as she continued to silently cry. I sat there, not saying a word. After a minute or two, she sat back up, wiping her face.

"Why did you do that?" she asked.

"Because you needed it," I said smiling. She smiled back at me. I stood up to leave.

"Abby?"

"Yeah?" I asked.

"How would you like spending tomorrow together, just me and you?"

"Really?" I asked.

She nodded.

"Um, yeah. I would really like that."

"I would too," she said, sounding like she actually meant it. "Well, you better get to bed."

"Yeah, sure. Well, goodnight."

"Goodnight."

I left the room and made my way back through the living room. Uncle Charles looked up from his book, saw my smile, and nodded.

"Goodnight, Abby."

"Goodnight!" I chirped.

I hurried up the stairs and shut my bedroom door. Jo was sitting on my bed, scrolling on her phone.

"Dad's taking up the whole bed," she muttered. "Mind if I camp out here for the night?"

"Sure," I shrugged. "I'll be right back."

I went to the bathroom to brush my teeth, wash my face, and put on pajamas. I was splashing my face with water, trying to rinse the soap off, when I heard a faint ticking sound. I dried my face with the towel and stood there, listening to the sound. I had never noticed a ticking sound before. I tiptoed down the hall, towards my room, where the ticking was getting louder. I opened the door to my room and fell forward, landing on damp grass. I wasn't in my room; I was back in the forest.

I stood up and wiped off my dirty hands, leaving a slight smear on the sides of my dress, and made my way down the hill slowly. The wind was blowing violently through the trees, causing the leaves to fly everywhere. I finally arrived at our secret place and saw the pile of stones lying between two trees. I knelt down and carefully moved the stones away, to reveal a hole with a black box nestled inside. It was covered in stickers, and had a dent on the side where I had dropped it once. My stomach muscles spasmed a little and I gasped as I placed my hand on my midsection. It had been a week since I'd been back home and my stomach was still tender. I opened the box and started going through its contents. There were pictures, a beautiful geode I had found when I was ten, a friendship bracelet, a hagstone, and my lucky rabbit's foot Gran had given me, and a carved wooden "love spoon" that I had been gifted to me. I pulled the ring from my pocket, gave it a kiss, and carefully placed it in the box. I knew it was too risky leaving it in the house for Mum or Dad to find.

I closed the lid to the box and placed it back into the hole. The stones were put back in the exact same order they had been in. I wasn't quite ready to go back home, so I decided to walk along the water for a bit. The water was a bit higher than usual with all of the recent rain, and was running a little faster than normal. As I walked, I felt the sudden urge to cry. I felt so isolated. All of my friends were off to college, my boyfriend gone for who knows how long, and my best friend was all the way on the other side of the ocean. My heart felt like it was being pulled in all directions.

Suddenly, something white floating down the stream caught my attention. As it passed, I realized it was a shoe; one that belonged to a little girl. I sprinted into the cold, thigh-deep water and snatched the shoe. I got out of the water and wrung out my clothes. The breeze picked up and goosebumps covered my skin. Wrapping my arms around myself, I kept walking upstream, hoping to find the owner of the missing shoe. I realized that I had never been this far into the woods before. I knew all I had to do was follow the stream back to familiar landscapes, but something in my gut told me to turn around and go back. It was getting dark and I, for some reason unknown to me, felt afraid. Up ahead, I could see a faint, glowing light low to the ground. Then, I heard the whistling.

Having an Irish mother and a British father, I had heard two lores. My dad told me about lantern men, while my mum insisted that the correct term was "will-o'-the-wisp." Either way, they were ghost lights that led a living person somewhere, usually to danger. My dad stopped believing in them as he grew older, but my mum still warned me to stay away from the ominous ghost lights. But seeing one in person for the first time, I was of course curious. I slowly moved further away from the stream, trying to get a better look at the light that bounced around in the dark forest. The ghostly whistling continued as the lantern man/will-o'-the-wisp moved through the trees. Finally, the light stopped moving and the whistling ceased.

I crouched down and crawled forward as I quickly realized that it was no ghost light; it was a man. I recognized him, but couldn't place his name. Something Henry, perhaps? I got down on my stomach and army-crawled forward a bit more. The flashlight he had been carrying was on the other side of him, so I could only make out shapes in the dark. One of the shapes was the man, but there was a smaller shape on the ground. I scooted forward on my elbows again and a branch dug into my arm before snapping under my weight. The man grabbed his flashlight and whipped around, trying to see where the noise had come from. I got down flat on my stomach, trying to lay as still as possible. I heard a faint whimper come from the direction of the man. He turned away and I slowly propped myself up.

The flashlight was carefully placed down next to the man, showing a little girl. From where I was, she looked to be anywhere from six to eight years old. And she was missing a shoe on her left foot. My heart started pounding. I slowly pulled my phone out of my pocket and looked at the screen. No service; but I wasn't surprised because I barely got any reception in my own house, let alone out in the dense woods. I looked up just as the man's enormous hands wrapped around the girl's throat. I put my hands tightly against my mouth to muffle my gasp. As I started using my feet to scoot back on my bottom, I heard the little girl cry out with a strange, squeaking sound. I paused long enough to see the man lift the little girl by the neck and slam her back down. Her head made a loud knock as it no doubt hit a rock. I let out a cry in terror and saw the man's head turn in my direction. I got up and sprinted back through the woods.

I followed the direction I was sure would lead me back to the stream as branches tore at my clothes and whipped me in the face. I didn't turn to see if the man was following me or not. If I somehow made it out of the woods, I was safe. Finally, I heard the familiar sound of rushing water and slowed down. I looked all around, holding my breath so I could hear any movement. The woods were silent besides the stream. I bent down and placed my hands on my knees, trying to catch my breath. Eventually, my breathing slowed and I stood back up. I felt a drop of rain hit my nose. I looked up at the dark sky. If only it could wait a little longer to rain, I thought. I started to make my way back to the house, closely sticking by the stream.

"Looks like a storm's coming," a shaky voice from behind me said.

I turned around to see a man standing in the trees.

5

I opened my eyes. I was back in my room, the smell of rain seeming far away now.

"Holy shit, Abby!"

I looked up at Jo's pale face from the floor.

"Did you just have a seizure?" she asked. "I'm getting Dad."

"Don't," I grabbed her arm. "I'm fine."

"The hell you are! You walked in, your eyes rolled back white, and you started falling forward. Luckily, I caught you in time. You were mumbling something but I couldn't understand you."

I sat up slowly and smacked my lips.

"I need a drink of water," I said, grabbing my throat.

Jo rushed over to the night stand and with shaking hands, picked up the glass of water. I took it from her and gulped the entire thing down. Jo took the glass from me as I panted and wiped the corner of my mouth.

"Do you think you can make it to the bed?" Jo asked. I nodded. Jo wrapped my arm around her neck and stood up. She sat me down slowly on the mattress and stood perfectly still, eyes fixed on me.

"So?" she asked. I sighed.

"I'm having...visions," I said slowly.

"What the hell does that mean?" Jo asked.

"I had one on the plane," I explained. "And then another in the car on the way here. I've had a couple since, but they're getting stronger, more vivid. This one seemed to last a half an hour."

"Abby, you were only unconscious for like a minute."

"Really?"

"C'mon. Tell me what's really going on. You haven't started drinking, have you?"

"Jo!"

"I'm just asking," she put her hands up defensively. "Look, I'll admit it. This place is...odd. I've felt it ever since we got here. And you and mom have been acting differently."

"How so?" I asked.

"Well for one, you've been a lot more chill. Less argumentative. And Mom hasn't drank once since the plane ride."

"Two whole days," I rolled my eyes. "Let's give her an award."

"I don't know. I think this place is changing her. Both of you."

I reached over and grabbed my journal and flipped through the pages.

"Look," I pointed to the grandfather clock picture. "I drew the room I'm staying in, and I hadn't seen it yet. Everything in the room is the exact same."

"Except for the clock," Jo pointed out.

"Yeah, I'm still not sure about that. But look at this."

I turned to the page of the woman dancing around the fairy ring.

"Damn, Abby, these are really good."

"Look at the last picture I drew before we left," I said as I showed her the drawing of the cat. "They're getting progressively better, and it's only been a few days," I breathed.

"This is kind of weird," Jo bugged her eyes out.

"I think..." I hesitated. "I'm being shown someone's life. Someone who might not be here anymore."

"What, like a ghost?" Jo chuckled.

"I know, I know. It sounds crazy."

"It sounds completely delusional and I don't think you should tell anyone else unless you want to be locked up in the loony bin."

My shoulders drop. Of course Jo didn't believe me.

"I'm confiding in you," I said, hurt. "You're my twin sister. I'm closer to you than anyone else in our family."

"Just imagine how close we'd be if you actually liked me," Jo said sharply.

"What's that supposed to mean? I love you."

"Of course you do. We're family. But We don't hang out at all."

"We live together," I smirked. "We see each other all the time."

"Yeah, but we don't actually spend time together. You're either in your room, alone, or out with your group of friends. You never want to do anything with me. You don't know anything about me."

"Oh please. I know so much about you."

"What's my favorite color?" Jo asked.

"Yellow."

"Wrong. It's teal. My favorite color hasn't been yellow since middle school. But that makes sense because that's when we started drifting apart."

"We started drifting apart because you were put in all of the honors classes," I corrected. "We never saw each other at school. And then we made our own separate friends who don't associate with each other."

"That's because your friends literally hate everyone who isn't in your friend group!" Jo snapped. "They're assholes!"

"Oh, I'm sorry my friends aren't super smart, pretentious douchebags."

"My friends accept me the way I am," Jo said as her eyes started tearing up. "I have to fake who I am at home and at school, and it's...exhausting. I can't even be myself fully around my twin sister. We're two halves of a whole and I feel like such a stranger to you."

"What could you possibly have to hide from everyone?" I asked. "You're the golden child. You don't argue with Mom and Dad. You make good grades and never get in trouble at school-"

"I'm gay," she blurted.

It felt like all of the air left the room. I held my breath and froze, unsure if I had heard my sister correctly. Jo put her face in her hands and started crying. I couldn't find the right words to say. I couldn't honestly say that I was shocked by the news; there were subtle hints throughout the years that I could have paid closer attention to. Jo never really talked about having crushes. Whenever I would ask her if an actor was cute, she'd shrug or say something like, "he's okay, I guess." Jo was never particularly feminine, and would say, "makeup and high heels are tools men pressure women to use to become living sex dolls." I thought it was her way of going against the norm. Mine was pink hair, nose piercing, heavy eyeliner, and listening to angsty music.

I placed my hands on Jo's shoulders and she looked up at me.

"Thank you for telling me that," I smiled. "I don't love you any less than I did a few minutes ago. In fact, knowing more about you makes me love you more. I'm always here if you need to talk to someone or just vent. I know I haven't done a great job of being there for you, so I promise to try and do better."

Jo lunged forward and wrapped her arms around my neck.

"I love you," I said softly.

"Love you too, Abby," she replied. "Please promise me that you won't say anything to Mom and Dad. I'm planning on telling them. I just want to wait for the right time."

"I won't say a word to anyone. It's not my business to tell."

Jo smiled at me.

"Thanks for telling me about your...issues you've been having," she added. "If you need to talk to me about anything, I'm here for you too."

"Thanks," I blushed. "Well, we should probably get some sleep. I'm exhausted."

We pulled back the blanket and got ourselves settled. Jo fell asleep almost immediately, but I tossed and turned. I wasn't lying when I said I was exhausted. But my mind was racing, and above all else, I felt uneasy; like I was constantly being watched.

The smell of food woke me up the next morning. I sat up, stretched and looked around. Since there were no windows in the room, I peeked at the light seeping in from under the door. Jo wasn't in the room, so I got up to make my bed and get dressed.

Then, I got my sketchbook out and quickly drew what I had seen in my last vision. I did a scribbled version of the shoe in the water at the top of the page, and then added the dark scene of the man hovering over a smaller, shadowed figure. I couldn't bring myself to draw details of the little girl because it made me sick to my stomach to think about. When I was done, I hid the journal under the bed and went downstairs.

The living room was empty; Uncle Charles' book he'd been reading lay on the arm of his chair with his pipe resting on top of it. I walked into the kitchen to find not Aunt Poppy cooking, but my sister. Jo was hovered over the stove; smoke coming up from two sizzling pans.

"Mmm, what's cooking?" I asked, mouth watering.

"Sausage, eggs, and I have biscuits in the oven."

"When did you become such a fine chef?"

"I took a cooking class last year, genius."

I stuck my tongue out at her.

"Do you need any help?" I asked, picking up a spatula.

"Flip the eggs for me," Jo commanded, taking two pieces of sausage off of one pan and setting them on a plate.

I carefully pushed the spatula under one egg. The white caught on the spatula, making a wrinkled mess of the egg. Trying to flip it, I ended up folding the egg instead.

"Oops."

"Here," Jo laughed. Taking my hand, she quickly shoved the spatula under the other egg and flipped it with ease.

"Uh, that one can be mine," I said, pointing to the folded egg. "Sorry I messed it up."

"It's okay. You'll get better with practice."

"Where is everyone, by the way?" I asked, picking at the splotches of dark blue polish left on my nails.

"They went down to the cemetery. I didn't want to go so I said I'd make breakfast for when they'd get back."

"I wonder when they'll be back. Mom and I had plans."

"What do you mean?" Jo asked as she pulled the biscuits out of the oven.

"Mom's taking me out for the day," I explained. Jo stopped where she was and turned to face me.

"You're kidding."

"Nope."

"Why?" she asked sharply.

"Why not?"

"You two don't ever get along. Ever. I at least don't talk back to her. Did she say anything about me?"

"No. You'll probably get to hang out with Dad."

"Great," Jo said, slamming the tray of biscuits down.

"What is the matter with you?" I asked, surprised by her reaction.

"Oh, nothing. I'm just so glad you and Mom are buddies now. Maybe she'll lay off of you and start hitting me when she drinks."

"Jo, please don't be like this. Don't be mad at me."

"I'm not mad at you," Her eyes filled with tears. "I'm mad at her."

"Jo-"

"Just leave me alone for a bit. Please."

I turned and went upstairs, trying to find something to do. Finally, I got out my guitar, tuned it, and started playing a few songs I had written. Even though I primarily listened to loud, angry music, I liked playing softer stuff on my guitar. I kind of mimicked my sound off of Phoebe Bridgers, my favorite female artist. I was in the middle of playing "Get On With It," when I heard a knock on my door. I got up and opened it, seeing my mom standing there. She was wearing a very large black floppy hat and a white sundress with big black polka dots on it.

"You do know that that outfit screams 'tourist,' right?"

She smiled at me saying, "It was the only thing I could find that made me look happy."

I wished my mom *was* happy, instead of just trying to look like it. She scowled at my choice of outfit: an oversized band shirt, long, baggy cargo shorts, and tennis shoes. My left shoe was developing a hole where my pinky toe was.

"Well, I'm glad I dressed up," my mom said sarcastically.

I looked down at my clothes.

"What did you expect? A frilly, pink dress with a bow in my hair?"

"You know," she whispered, "I think that's just what you need."

"What exactly is that supposed to mean?"

"You need some girl clothes, Abby."

"These *are* girl clothes!" I said tugging on my shirt. "I bought these in the junior girl's department. Besides, I'm a girl and I'm wearing them, making them girl clothes."

"I just wish you'd stop dressing like Billie Eilish."

"What's wrong with Billie Eilish?" I asked, crossing my arms. "If you had it your way, I'm sure you'd rather I dress more like Ariana Grande."

"Now, she is a doll! So glamorous and feminine!"

"I don't want to be glamorous or feminine, Mom. You're the one who looks good in glam. I want to be comfortable."

I could see a slight smile start to form on my mom's mouth. She knew she looked good. She was in good shape, had no gray hair, and hardly any wrinkles. She could possibly get away with being my older sister. Perks of having kids way too young, I supposed. I pulled at my baggy shorts.

"This is comfortable for me."

My mom turned to face me. She took a few steps closer to me and put her hand on my shoulder. I flinched as she did and she moved her hand away.

"I know this is comfortable for you," she said. "But would it kill you to do something for me just once? Just let me buy you some new clothes."

"Do something for *you*?" I scoffed, putting my hands on my hips. "Why should I? Give me one good reason. You've never done anything for me."

My mom carefully walked into my room, as if she were afraid something would jump out at her, and sat down on my bed.

"Abby, I know I haven't been the best mom, by far. I know I've done some things to you that were really..."

"Shitty," I finished, sitting down next to her.

"Uh. Well, yeah. Yeah, you're right. I just want you to know that, um, I never meant to hurt you."

"You never meant to slap me or call me a bitch?" I asked, looking her straight in the eye. She turned away from me.

"Look, Abby, I'm not good at this whole apologizing thing. Just know that I didn't do the things I did to hurt you. I thought it might just take away some of my own pain, instead of adding more to your life."

"What could have possibly happened that made you hit your own child? Just because your cousin died a long time ago, doesn't mean you have to make my-"

"You don't know half the things I have gone through, Abby."

"How could I if you never talk to me? You've pushed Jo and me away for so long that it's like strangers living together. All I wanted growing up was the typical family experiences. Board game nights, going to the movies together, Sunday morning breakfasts, family vacations; and I know we're on one right now, but why has it taken sixteen years? Are you and Dad doing badly, like financially?"

"I, I just-" my mom stammered. "I just never..."

I knew what she wanted to say. She never wanted children. I stood up and, without looking at my mom, walked out of my room. As I reached for the bathroom door, I paused, suddenly realizing something. I was afraid to go into the bathroom. I withdrew a deep breath. I exhaled and turned the doorknob slowly. The door whined as it opened. I flipped on the light switch as soon as I could get my arm in.

Not looking around at anything, I scurried across the creaking tile. I reached the sink and grabbed my toothbrush with a trembling hand. I opened the medicine cabinet to get the toothpaste. I fumbled around, knocking over bottles and tubes of different things. A pill bottle fell on the floor with a tiny smack. I bent down to pick it up, and read it as I was returning it to the cabinet:

> Amitriptyline
> Anti-Depressant
> Poppy Murray, to be taken twice a day, every day

I quickly placed the bottle back into its original spot and grabbed the tube of toothpaste. Aunt Poppy was on medication because she was still depressed about her daughter, even after all of this time. The woman, who seemed so happy about every little thing, was really in pain. I began brushing my teeth, thinking how weird I thought Aunt Poppy was when I met her. I bent over to spit out the excess foam and spit into the sink. I stood up and wiped my mouth. My eyes widened and my mouth tried to make a sound, although nothing escaped. In the mirror's reflection, I could see someone standing behind me. It was a little girl, the side of her head was caved in and there was dried blood down to her shoulder. Her milky eyes stared up at me in the reflection as her mouth opened to scream. I turned quickly, knocking the tube of toothpaste off the sink. However, when I faced the wall, nothing was there. I rubbed my eyes and tried again. Nothing. Everything looked normal.

"I must be losing my damn mind," I chuckled to myself through a shaken voice. I quickly put the toothpaste and toothbrush where they belong and ran out of the bathroom. I skipped every other step and hopped down on the landing, into the living room where Aunt Poppy was drinking a cup of tea. She looked up at me and smiled.

"Your mum just went outside. Said she'd be back in a few."

I nodded and sat down in the chair Uncle Charles usually sat in. I noticed the pipe was gone, however, the smell was still there, like it was permanently in the leather.

"Went to play cards with some friends," said Aunt Poppy, knowing what I was about to ask. "Took your dad and sister with him."

70

I nodded again.

"Are you alright, dear? You're trembling."

I put my shaking hands into the pockets of my shorts and smiled.

"Just a bit cold, that's all," I lied.

Aunt Poppy looked at me above her glasses. I turned away to look at the collection of books on the shelves. I noticed a book of poetry, a book about old car models, and a line of cook books. There was a row of more odd books; ones about paganism, worshiping nature, honoring The Goddess, and using herbs and brews correctly. The rest were works of fiction. The front door opened suddenly, causing me to jump, and my mom stumbled in. At first I was afraid she had been drinking, but then I noticed the heel on one of her shoes had broken off.

"Damn shoes," she swore and hobbled in.

"Where did you go?" asked Aunt Poppy.

"Um, nowhere. Just walked around." She turned towards me. "Let me go get another pair of shoes and we'll head out, okay?"

I smiled and nodded once more.

"Are you slowly becoming mute?" Aunt Poppy asked.

I shook my head smiling. We both giggled at this.

"Really, why are you so quiet all of a sudden?"

"I don't know," I shrugged. "I guess I don't have much to say."

"A Roman politician once wisely said, 'I will begin to speak when I have that to say which had not better be unsaid.'"

I stared at her, waiting for her to explain what that meant. Instead, she sipped her cup of tea, swirled it a bit, poured a little onto her saucer, and looked into the cup intensely.

"What're you doing?" I asked.

"Reading," Aunt Poppy said, concentrating on something in the cup.

I gave her a puzzled look as she continued looking in the cup. My mom came back out, wearing denim shorts, a white blouse, a beige cardigan, and sandals. I was so envious how my mom could make every outfit she wore look good.

"You ready?" Mom asked. I nodded.

We said goodbye to Aunt Poppy and got into the rental car.

"Jo was pissed you didn't invite her with us today," I said as my mom backed out of the driveway.

"I figured she wouldn't want to come," my mom raised her eyebrows. "A shopping day didn't really seem like her thing."

"Wait, so no one's staying with Aunt Poppy?" I looked up the driveway at the house.

"I'm sure she'll find something to do to keep herself out of trouble."

After that, neither of us spoke for the next thirty minutes. I was beginning to get curious.

"Where exactly are we going to shop?" I asked, breaking the silence.

"Well, you mentioned London on our first day here."

I glanced quickly at my mom, who flashed a smile.

"You're kidding!"

"It's not like Effingham would have anything good," she snickered.

I couldn't believe I was going to get to shop in London, England. This vacation was finally starting to feel like a vacation. The rest of the drive to London, my mom and I talked; we talked about music, movies, food, and new trends.

"I don't know how kids can stand having their noses pierced like that. They look like bulls. Wouldn't that hurt?"

"It's called a septum piercing, Mom. Actually, my friend Motley said his didn't hurt at all."

My mom started laughing.

"What?" I asked.

"Is his last name Crue?" she asked, laughing even harder.

I rolled my eyes and smiled.

"Where do people come up with these names?" My mom wiped her eyes.

I shrugged, shaking my head. As we entered London, I started getting anxious. My mom parked on the side of a road in front of a bakery. We got out of the car and I looked in the window at all of the tasty looking treats.

"Mom," I nodded towards the bakery. "Can we get something?"

"Not right now," she said. "Come on."

I sighed as I caught up to her to cross the street. We walked around the corner on King Street, and I saw a big building.

"Is that a mall?" I asked. "Is this it?"

"This is it."

My mom opened the door and I trailed closely behind. The store smelled very clean, which fit the store itself well. The walls, the shelves, the counters, and the floor were all pearly white. Most of the clothes were either beige, black, or white, were folded very carefully, and were mostly suits.

"Mom, you can't be serious," I said, nervous.

"Don't worry, we're just cutting through this store to get to yours."

"May I help you?" said a deep, sharp voice.

I turned to face a tall, thin woman who was, of course, wearing a suit and high heels. She was also wearing so much makeup, if I ran a finger across her cheek, I'm sure it would come off like icing on a cake. She had narrow, pointy eyes and a large mole on the side of her chin. I noticed her curled, red hair stacked on top of her head like a beehive. Her name tag said, HELEN.

"Just passin' through, ma'am," I said in a thick, Southern accent.

"Come on," my mom pulled on my shirt sleeve and led me out of the store. I turned one last time to Helen and saluted her. She scoffed and turned away.

"Why do you have to be like that?" my mom asked as we exited the hoity-toity store.

"What?" I asked. "Why do I like to have fun and make pretentious, stuck-up people uncomfortable? Because the world

73

would be a lot better if people like that didn't have a stick up their butts."

"Honestly, I don't know what to do with you sometimes."

"Just let me be myself?"

My mom shook her head in disapproval and we made our way to a store called Primark. It looked promising at first. They had plenty of oversized band shirts and baggy pants. But my mom kept showing me a bunch of tiny shirts, skirts, and dresses.

"Mom, I don't know if these will even cover my a-"

"Hi, can I help you?"

A young woman with short bleach-blonde hair came up and smiled at us, showing a gap between her front teeth.

"We're looking for some new clothes for my daughter," my mother explained.

The woman looked at me, staring down at my dirty, once white tennis shoes, at my baggy shorts, past my two-sizes-too-large shirt, up to my uncombed, dyed hair in a ponytail. She grinned a wide grin at me.

"We have plenty of items in her style!" she squealed. "I love the alternative look!"

"We're trying to branch out to something more...feminine," my mom explained.

"Ah, gotcha."

"I'll be right back," my mom said, turning to me.

"You're leaving me?" I asked, sounding panicked.

"I won't be long," she smiled. "I just need to go check in with the salon about your appointment."

"Salon?" I repeated.

"We'll start with some new clothes and then move onto hair. I also want you to get some new makeup."

"Moooomm," I groaned.

"It'll be fun," she winked. "I promise."

6

After my mom left, the store employee, who I learned was named Kate, hooked her arm in mine and dragged me through the rows of clothes. I was immediately overstimulated by how muggy the store was, how much Kate was talking, the blaring pop music playing, and the clothes thrown in my face.

"Do you know what your mother is wanting specifically?" Kate asked, rummaging through hanging clothes.

"Something to show off my girlish figure," I replied, mimicking my mom's tone. "But I don't want to look like a skank."

Kate chuckled.

"Alright, less 'baddie' aesthetic and more 'flirty' feminine."

"Sure," I said, even though I wasn't actually sure.

Kate shoved a thick pile of clothes into my hands; I could barely see over the top of the pile. She directed me into an empty dressing room. Inside the room was a large mirror and wooden bench. I picked the first piece, a pastel blue baby doll dress, and hung everything else up on the hooks inside the dressing room. I pulled off my shirt and put the dress on over the shorts. I opened and shut the door quickly but Kate's hand caught it and opened it all the way.

"Ohhh! You look- wait, is that a sports bra? Do you still have your shorts on?"

"It's a little short," I blushed, tugging at the dress.

Kate lifted up my dress.

"Hey!" I shouted.

"Take the shorts off so we can get a better idea of what it looks like on you!"

Reluctantly, I pulled down the shorts, cupping my hands around my buttcheeks.

"The dress is a little short on you," Kate said, tapping an index finger to her lips. "But we definitely need to do something about the bra to get a better idea of what we're working with. Come on."

I followed Kate to the back wall of the store, pulling on the bottom of my dress as I walked. I stopped to face a wall of lingerie.

"Oh God," I whispered.

Kate grabbed a bra and held it up to my chest.

"Kind of hard to tell what size you need when you have them smashed down."

"C34," I muttered. I was so embarrassed.

Kate snatched a couple of bras, led me back to the dressing room, and told me to continue trying on outfits.

I went back in, grabbed a skirt and shirt, and put them on.

"How darling!" Kate cried as I came out.

I had on a pleated green and black plaid skort (a skirt with built-in shorts) and a cropped black tank top.

"With the built-in shorts, you don't have to worry about anything showing," Kate explained. "And the black top will go with multiple bottoms we pick out. I figured we could do two basic tops, two patterned, two basic bottoms, and two patterned. That way you can mix them up to have several different outfits!"

My mom came back just as I was trying on one more dress. Kate described it as a "mini tea dress," with a squared neck and capped sleeves. It was black with cherries on it, and I actually really liked it on me.

"Did we pick out something other than black clothes?" my mom sighed.

"Don't worry, I made sure we had some color in there," Kate winked and pointed to my outfits.

"Oh, thank goodness," Mom sighed. "Okay, well get changed so I can pay for everything. We need to get to your hair appointment."

I nodded and quickly got back into my clothes. I took the dress up to the register and my mom handed me a brown paper sack. I looked inside and there were several pastries from the bakery we had passed.

"I wasn't sure what you wanted, so I grabbed a few things," my mom smiled. "Figured we could snack while you get your hair done."

"Thank you!" I exclaimed, hugging her. She slowly patted my back.

"Abby, it's just some eclairs, tarts, and cookies."

I was dreading getting my hair done, but the surprise goodies from my mom made it a little better. We walked next door to the salon. As we walked through the door, a short man with a French accent cried out, "Ah, Maggie!"

He was bald with a pink beard and matching pink eyebrows. He had on a coral tank top that said, "No Bad Vibes" and white capris. He ran over, clapping his hands.

"Is this the daughter?" he asked. "She looks like a sister!"

"Oh, thank you," my mom blushed, playfully swatting her hand.

"My name is Chase, and I am here to help transform you into the best version of yourself," he said, holding his hand out to me. I went to shake it, but he lifted my hand to his face and gave it a kiss. "I'm going to make sure you're taken care of and walk out of here happy, okay?"

I nodded and followed Chase to a seat in front of one of the sinks. I tilted my head back and Chase turned on the faucet. He scrubbed and scrubbed until I thought my hair was going to fall out. First, he used a smoothing shampoo. Then, he added a sweet-smelling conditioner. Last, he rinsed my hair and wrung it out. After washing my hair, Chase led me over to the seat where he cut it. Strands fell clumps onto the ground around me.

"What exactly are you doing to my hair?" I asked.

"Layering, texturing, and cutting off all of the split ends," explained Chase, snipping off more hair.

After Chase had cut my hair exactly the way he wanted it cut, he started mixing the hair dye in a bowl.

"I'm going to color your hair back to its natural dark blonde and then do a platinum money piece in the front. So cute for summertime!"

I had no idea what a money piece was, so I just nodded and let him do his thing. Applying the dye took about ten minutes. My mom distributed the goodies from the bakery, and even shared with Chase. My favorite was the lemon tart. I had never had something so fresh and "melt-in-your-mouth" delicious. After Chase washed out the dye and dried my hair, he took me back over to the sink. Chase led me to a chair and leaned me back. He started applying thick, hot goop to the area right below my eyebrows. He then added a long, white strip of paper that stuck to the goop.

"You might want to count to three on this one," said Chase.

"Um, okay. One, two-"

Chase ripped off the paper strip and it felt like he took a layer of skin off. I let out a loud howl and jumped out of the chair.

"God damn! Are you crazy?" I shouted.

"Please, sit back down!" Chase pleaded, sitting me back down. "We still have the left one and the middle one!"

"You mean I have to do this two more times?" I asked, rubbing my sore eye.

"We will do it in a hurry, no?"

"Fine, whatever."

I gripped the arms of the chair and took in a deep breath. Chase pulled off the strip on the left. I yelped in pain and told him to quickly do the other one. Chase removed the strip in the middle and I winced. My eyebrows felt like they were on fire.

"How can girls do this to themselves?"

"At least you didn't get a bikini wax," Chase chuckled, emphasizing each syllable so it came out, "bee-kee-nee."

After the swelling in my face went down, Chase got to work on makeup. He taught me about primer, concealer, and all of the different brushes used for different products. After makeup, Chase grabbed my cherry dress from my mom so I could show off the whole look. After I changed, I spotted a full-length mirror in the corner of the salon and slowly walked in front of it. I was looking at my reflection, but it felt like I was looking at a completely different person. Instead of dark, baggy clothes, I was wearing a dress. Instead of long, hot pink hair, my hair was blonde and layered, just at my shoulders. Two bright blonde streaks framed my face, and Chase had curled some parts, showing off the layers. Instead of heavy eyeliner on a pale, blotchy face, I had smooth, healthy skin with natural-looking makeup and shaped eyebrows. Chase came up behind me smiling.

"You look so pretty! I want to just cry."

"Thank you," I replied, eyes tearing.

"You're not allowed to cry! You can't ruin my masterpiece!"

I laughed as he walked me to the front lobby where my mom was sitting. Chase cleared his throat and my mom's jaw dropped when she looked up.

"Oh my god," she gasped.

Chase giggled and twirled me around so my mom could see all of me. She suddenly started crying.

"What's wrong?" I asked.

"You look absolutely stunning."

I blushed.

"I love you just the way you are," she continued. "But you're becoming a young woman and I want you to know that your value is more than just your appearance. But I also want you to have confidence and to try new looks while you're still figuring out who you want to be. If you don't like the hair by the end of summer, you can dye it pink again."

"But no more box color!" Chase scolded. "Get it done professionally, please."

I laughed and promised I would. My mom and I left the salon and headed to a music store I had seen in the mall. I noticed Aunt Poppy And Uncle Charles had a record player so I grabbed a few albums that looked interesting and paid.

When we were back in Effingham, my mom decided she was going to stop by a handmade jewelry store that Aunt Poppy recommended. I noticed as we slowed down in front of the store that we were across the street from Trotter's, the cafe where Rachel and Callum worked. My mom caught me staring.

"Are you okay?" My mom asked.

"The boy I met the night I ran off works over there."

She looked towards the restaurant and nodded.

"Why don't you go over and talk to him? Ask him how he's been."

"No!" I shouted.

"Why not?"

"He has a girlfriend."

"Is that where those clothes came from?"

"No, those are Rachel's; his sister's."

My mom nodded slowly. We looked around at the jewelry for a while until my mom picked out a pair of earrings. We were getting back into the car when my mom abruptly said, "Tomorrow, you're going to return Rachel's clothes, and if Callum is there, you're going to talk to him and show him what he's missing."

"Um, no thanks."

"You can't just steal someone's clothes, Abby."

"I'll just quickly leave the clothes on the counter and Rachel can take them whenever she sees them after I leave."

"Oh, that's brave of you," my mom said sarcastically.

As we pulled into the driveway, Aunt Poppy's head popped up from the garden. She waved at us with a freshly dug carrot swinging in her hand. I stepped out of the car and she gasped. The carrot dropped from her hand and she ran over to hug me tight.

"You look just breathtaking," she played with my hair. "And you look like such a young lady!"

I withstood the five minutes of comments from Aunt Poppy, then the three of us made our way into the house.

My dad, Jo, and Uncle Charles were sitting in the living room talking and drinking tea. They all stopped to stare at me. My cheeks burned from embarrassment.

"Abby, I didn't hardly recognized you," Uncle Charles said before taking a puff from his pipe.

"Whoa!" Jo said loudly. "Look who's all trendy and girly now."

I couldn't tell if she was giving me a hard time or if she actually liked my new look.

"I don't like it," my dad said sternly. We all looked at him. He had his arms crossed and his eyes were narrow.

"What do you mean?" I asked. "You don't like the dress?"

"No, I don't like any of it. I don't like how skimpy the dress is, I don't like the hair color, and I don't like all of the makeup. Why are your..." He pointed to his own chest. "...so much bigger? What did you do to her?" He faced my mom, who stood there with her mouth gaped.

"Excuse me? I didn't do anything to her."

"You took my daughter and turned her into what you want her to be. Just let her be herself!"

"She still is herself!" my mom yelled back. "And she's *our* daughter. I just thought it would be fun to-"

"To what? Treat her like your personal doll to dress up? She looks way older than sixteen, and I'm not okay with it."

"She seems alright, she's not complaining."

"Yeah," scoffed my dad. "You're actually showing her attention, and in a positive way. I wouldn't complain either. And I know I'm not supposed to be saying anything, but I think what you're doing is wrong. I'm tired of lying to both of them!"

My dad grabbed his jacket that was hanging by the door and walked out. Jo walked over to me and put her arm around me. It was unusual for both of us to see our dad act like that. Usually Mom was the one who had the emotional outbursts while Dad was the calm, collected one.

"Well, I think you look pretty," Mom said sharply.

"I think she looks like her mother," Uncle Charles snickered as he took another puff.

"If you don't like the clothes, we can take them back," my mom added before storming off.

"How about I get my mattress and put it in your room, and we can have a little campout tonight, like when we were little," Jo suggested. I nodded, smiling weakly.

"I'm going to put something more comfortable on," I said softly.

I went up to my room and turned on the lights. I put on some basketball shorts, a pair of fuzzy socks, and a t-shirt. I turned around and my jaw dropped when I noticed what was standing in the corner. I quickly ran out of the room and down the stairs. My sudden reappearance startled everyone.

"What is that in my room?" I was out of breath.

"Honey, what's wrong?" Aunt Poppy asked. "You asked about one and we had one stored in the basement. So, I thought I'd put it in your room."

"What's she talking about?" my mom reappeared, asking Aunt Poppy.

"Remember when I was showing the kids their rooms the first day you were here? And Abigail mentioned something about a grandfather clock. I thought it was quite odd she had made such a request, but I was home alone all day today and thought to myself, 'Why not do something nice for Abigail?' So I called one of the neighbors to help me move it to her room. You don't like it?"

"I can't believe you, Poppy," Uncle Charles chimed in, shaking his head.

"What?" she asked him.

"You put Olivia's clock back, and you're acting like it's no big deal."

"That's because it isn't," Aunt Poppy said. "If you-"

"Wait!" I yelled. "I've been staying in Olivia's room? No wonder I've been having so many weird things happening to me."

"What do you mean?" my mom asked.

"I've been.. experiencing... things."

"What the hell are you talking about?" Mom raised her voice.

"This place- more specifically my room...is haunted."

"*Abigail*!" Mom hissed.

"*It is*! There's a ghost in the house and it's only been contacting me, probably because I'm the only one staying in her room!"

My mother's hand reached out like a whip and cracked across my face. With one moment, one decision, my mom had completely undone our perfect day together.

"Margaret!" cried Aunt Poppy.

"Mom!" cried Jo.

My mom stared at me, not moving and with no look of remorse on her face. My bottom lip started to tremble and I ran upstairs before I started to cry. I quickly washed the makeup off in the bathroom. I rubbed my stinging cheek and wiped away the tears. When I got back to my room, I pulled my hoodie on and crawled into bed. I stared at the grandfather clock and realized the hands hadn't moved. It wasn't working. There was a knock on the door that startled me.

"Go away!" I yelled.

"Abby, it's me," Jo's voice called softly.

"I don't want to be around anyone, Jo. Not even you."

"Mom just left. As soon as Dad walked back in, Mom took the rental car."

"Probably off to the closest bar," I mumbled.

"C'mon, let me come in," Jo pleaded.

I sighed heavily and slowly made my way to the door. As soon as I opened it, Jo came in and hugged me.

"I can't believe she hit you in front of Aunt Poppy and Uncle Charles," Jo said in disbelief.

"Doesn't surprise me at all," I replied. "I knew today was too good to be true."

I got my sketch journal out from under the bed and sat back on the mattress. Jo was staring at the grandfather clock.

"I'm not making stuff up and you know it," I lowered my voice. "There's something weird going on."

"I know, I believe you."

Jo grabbed my hand and suddenly, the room disappeared around me.

"Looks like a storm's coming."
I turned around to see a man standing in the trees.

83

"Oh," I said, startled. "Yeah, a storm."

The man standing in front of me smiled. He looked familiar, I knew I had seen him before. He had a vintage polaroid camera around his neck and beads of sweat on his forehead twinkled in the moonlight.

"I live in town," the man said. "My name is Seamus. Seamus Harvey? I've seen you, you know. I've watched you grow up into this beautiful woman. You have another little girl visit every summer. Although I haven't seen her in quite some time."

"It's...my cousin. She used to visit every summer but hasn't since my aunt died."

I watched as the man started walking slowly towards me. I had a very uneasy feeling in my stomach.

"Well, I better be going," I backed up and turned away from him. "I have some things at home to do."

"What? To feed your baby?"

I stopped and faced him again.

"It must be exhausting, being a teenage mother. I have two kids of my own. Of course I'm married and older than you. Much, much older than you."

"Yeah, I'm lucky to have my parents," I said, laughing awkwardly. "Speaking of, they're probably worried about me."

I turned to walk away once more.

"Who's the father?" he asked. "Or do you even know?"

"Yes, I know who-"

I stopped. The man was smiling even bigger now. I looked down to see that this much older man was now obviously aroused. I wanted to scream for help but I knew no one would hear. I felt hopeless. I turned to run, and the man ran after me, twice as fast as I was. He reached out and grabbed a handful of my hair, pulling me down to the ground. My left temple hit a rock as I landed, and I felt the side of my head split open. I looked up to see the man that had thrown me down, sneering at me.

"Who would have thought that such a good little girl was a whore?"

I started crying and he leaned in, smelling me. Then, he slowly ran his tongue from my jaw to my temple. His breath was sour and hot against my skin.

"Please don't hurt me," I whimpered.

"I know you saw me," he gritted his teeth and grabbed my face roughly.

"Please, I promise I won't tell anyone! Just let me go. I promise I won't say anything.

"Oh, I know you won't," he laughed. "I'll make sure of that!"

Terror flooded over me as Seamus Harvey grabbed me by my hair again and dragged me deeper into the woods.

My eyes fluttered open and I was back in my room.

"Oh thank god," Jo sighed. "Abby, this is some seriously weird shit."

I looked down and realized I had taken up two pages of my journal with another drawing. There was the stream and a woman laying on the ground. She was face down on a rock with blood coming out of her head. A man was standing over her, except he was huge in the picture; an over exaggerated size for a normal man. He had black eyes and fangs, portraying the monster he really was.

"Your eyes rolled back and you started drawing," Jo explained.

"And you didn't call for help or anything?" I asked.

"I...don't think we should."

"Why?" I asked.

"Obviously, something is trying to communicate with you. Maybe there's a reason why."

"Uncle Charles did say that they never found their daughter," I remarked. "Maybe these visions will somehow give me the answer."

Jo nodded.

"What?" I asked, noticing the look on Jo's face.

"I just want you to be careful," Jo said. "I'm not a psychic or anything, but I have a weird feeling."

"I'll be fine," I said. "Even if Seamus Harvey did do something to Mom's cousin, he can't do anything to me. He's been dead for years."

"Still," Jo said, grabbing her stomach. "I have a feeling."

I helped Jo bring her mattress into my room and laid it across the floor. Jo insisted on sleeping in there in case anything else happened. She went downstairs to tell everyone goodnight, but I stayed in the room. When she came back, we talked until we couldn't keep our eyes open any longer.

I could hear the grandfather clock ticking loudly in the corner and my eyes slowly opened. Jo's snoring told me it was still night time. I reached down to pick up my journal, however, I couldn't feel it under my bed anywhere. I felt around some more and my hand landed on something else. Something soft and bumpy. I pulled out a dusty rugby ball. There was a name written on it but I couldn't tell what it said.

"What the-"

I hopped off the bed, turned on the flashlight on my phone, and got down on the floor. Jo turned over in her sleep, but didn't wake. I lifted the bed skirt and looked underneath. I could only see a few boxes. A couple of the boxes were round. I pulled one out and opened it. Inside was a stack of hats that I would never wear. One was a short, green bowl-looking hat. Another almost looked like an orange lobster. Who would wear these ugly things? I continued to look at the odd hats until I got to the bottom. In the bottom of the box were folded papers. I unfolded them and found what looked like to be drawings of more hats.

My mom's cousin was really into hats, apparently, I thought. I continued to dig things out from under the bed. I came across a pair of tap-dancing shoes, a record of the Bee Gees, and an old yearbook. I grabbed it and hopped back onto my bed to look through it.

I flipped through pages of black and white pictures filled with never-aging high school faces. Some were playing sports, some were at dances, and some were just going through everyday high school life. I started looking through the student pictures, looking at the different posed smiles.

Ding.

The large grandfather clock started to chime, letting me know it was midnight. The first chime startled me and the yearbook slipped from my grasp and fell on the floor with a loud smack.

Ding.

I froze as Jo snored abruptly and then sighed in her sleep.

Ding.

I bent down to close the yearbook and pushed it back under my bed.

Ding.

I heard something scrape against the floor on the other side of the bed as everything shifted.

Ding.

I peeked down on the other side to see a small black box; one similar to the one in my vision from the plane. There was an etching of a celtic-looking tree on the top.

Ding.

I picked it up and turned it over. There was a small, silver padlock on it. The key for the lock had to have been the size of a quarter.

Ding.

I looked over at the clock standing in the corner, covering my ears as the seventh ding chimed. I could've sworn it was getting louder. I carried the black box over to the clock.

Ding.

I reached for the long cabinet door on the bottom of the clock.

Ding.

I opened it and carefully placed the box in the bottom of the dust and cobwebs.

Ding.

I suddenly realized that I had done what the vision of the clock showed me. And then I looked at Jo.

Ding.

I grabbed my sketchbook and flipped to the page that had the drawing of the clock. It was the exact same one that was in the room before me. The twelfth ding told me that it was also the final one. I closed the journal and put it away. This was all beginning to feel like a huge puzzle I was supposed to solve. I went to bed, wondering if I should talk to Olivia about my visions. I could go talk to her after I dropped off Rachel's clothes when I woke up. My only explanation was absurd though.

What would I even say? "Yeah so I found out that I had an aunt with the same name as you, who died around your age who has been haunting my dreams, telling me her story, scaring the hell out of me every time I go in the bathroom, and I think she might be haunting you too because she wants us to solve her possible murder." How could I say any of that without sounding like a complete basket case?

I woke up the next morning to knocking on my door. I turned over, away from the door and tried to ignore the noise.

"Abigail, are you up?"

"Abby, it's Abby for crying out loud," I mumbled before raising my voice. "Yes, Aunt Poppy. I'm up now!"

"Good! Hurry up, get dressed, and come downstairs."

I sat up, stretched a bit, and went downstairs, still in my basketball shorts and hoodie. Jo was sitting on the couch, dark circles under her eyes. My dad was sitting next to her doing another crossword puzzle.

"Did the clock wake you up too?" I asked.

Uncle Charles was reading the day's newspaper and smoking his tobacco pipe. He looked up at me.

"What are you talking about?" Jo asked. "That clock doesn't work. You *were*, however, talking in your sleep almost all night and kept waking me up."

Aunt Poppy came in from the kitchen and motioned for me to sit down. My mom came in behind her.

"Abigail, Joanna, I want to talk to the both of you," Aunt Poppy sighed.

"Can't we do this some other time?" my mom asked.

"I agree," I said. "I need to go into town and take care of something."

The smile on Aunt Poppy's face disappeared.

"Margaret…" she said.

"We have all summer for family discussions. Let the girls go have fun for now."

Aunt Poppy hung her head.

"Jo, go with her," Mom added. "You need to get out of the house."

"But Mom, I-"

"Jo, just go with her."

Jo groaned and slowly got up from the couch. I followed her to the stairs and was stopped by my dad.

"Hey, kiddo," he said softly. "I'm- I'm sorry about last night."

"It's fine," I responded casually.

"I know you're a teenager now and you are going to be an adult before I know it. You're already old enough to drive and start dating…I don't know. I just still see you two as little girls and I guess I blinked."

I smiled.

"Your hair looks nice," he said.

"Thanks."

"And I shouldn't have walked out last night when I got upset," he added. "I promise I'll never do it again."

"It's okay, Dad. Really."

He smiled at me and gave me a hug. I quickly got dressed and did my makeup. I put one of my new tops on with a pair of jean shorts. The shorts were originally supposed to go to mid-thigh, but since I was wearing a dusty rose cami, I decided to cuff my shorts another couple of inches. I had to wear my dirty white tennis shoes, because we hadn't bought any new shoes. I grabbed Rachel's stuff before heading downstairs and making my way towards the door.

"Come on, Jo!" I called.

"Hold on!" I heard her yell.

"Cute outfit."

I turned to face my mom, who was now the only one sitting in the living room.

"Um, thanks."

"Did you get those shorts yesterday?" she asked.

"I just cuffed them," I said, shaking my head.

"We should have gotten you some new shoes."

I nodded.

"What size do you wear?"

"Eight, most of the time. With socks, eight and a half."

"Me too," my mom murmured.

I stood there, waiting for her to say something next.

"If you ever want to borrow a pair of my shoes, you can."

"Thanks," I replied. "Same goes for you too."

Before she could say anything else, I stepped out the door to wait for Jo. She finally came out, wearing black bike shorts, a white cropped tank top, and-

"Is that one of Dad's shirts?" I asked.

She nodded, laughing. She did a spin and the orange, blue, and green Hawaiin shirt that Mom had complained about for so long twirled around her.

"You know," I said, "the whole lesbian thing is starting to make sense now."

"Oh shut up," Jo laughed. "Let's go."

It felt like it took a lot longer to get there and was warmer than the first time. It was beginning to feel like summer. On our way to the café, we passed the same man with his flock of sheep as when we first arrived a couple of weeks ago. He waved to us and we waved back. *People like you more when you blend in more*, I thought to myself, looking down at my outfit. We walked down the main street of Effingham and before turning on the café's street, I looked at my reflection in a store window. I adjusted my bra, pulled up my top a little, and ran my fingers through my hair. We approached the front door to Trotter's. I took a deep breath and reached for the door.

7

We walked through the cafe's front door and my legs suddenly felt too heavy to move. I just needed to make it to the counter, set the clothes down, and walk out. I looked around at the waiters and waitresses. None of them looked like Rachel or Callum. I made my way towards the counter.

"Hi, how many?" a waitress stopped and asked us.

"Oh, we're not here to eat actually," I said hurriedly.

"Would you like something to drink?"

"Uh, um no."

"Are you okay? You look a little flushed."

"No thanks. Just dropping something off for Rachel," I explained quickly. She nodded, smiled, and walked off.

I sat the clothes down and turned towards the door.

"Callum thought you would come back to return those."

I stopped where I was and turned around to face Rachel with her arms crossed. She was wearing a black halter dress with a red t-shirt under it and red knee-length socks.

"Hey, Rachel," I waved awkwardly.

"Took you long enough."

"Sorry," I avoided eye contact.

"Who's this?"

She nodded towards Jo, who looked more like a deer caught in the headlights than I did.

"This is my twin sister, Jo," I said.

Rachel moved her eyes up and down Jo and smirked.

"He's not here, by the way. Went a few doors down to get more bread."

I nodded slowly.

"He wants to see you," she added.

"I don't think that would be a good idea," I tugged on my shirt a little.

"Why not?" asked Rachel.

"Selene," I answered quietly. "I don't think his girlfriend would like that too much."

Rachel slowly uncrossed her arms and a wide grin spread across her face.

"Go downstairs."

"What?" I asked, surprised.

"Just go down there and wait for him to get back. There's a lot that needs to be explained."

I turned to Jo.

"I can wait here," she shrugged.

"Are you sure?" I asked.

"Don't worry," Rachel winked. "I'll look after Jo. Make sure she stays out of trouble. Just go down there where you two can have some privacy to discuss things."

I gave Jo a sympathetic look and hesitantly went down to their basement apartment. Not knowing where exactly to sit, since there was stuff covering the couch, I paced the floor while I waited for Callum to come back. I looked around at the different pictures on the shelves. There were several of Callum and Rachel together. There was one particularly cute photo of them from Halloween years ago. Callum was dressed as Tigger and Rachel as Piglet. There was a photograph of them with an elderly couple; their grandparents, I'd guessed. Then, there was a polaroid picture of a man, a woman, a little boy, and a baby. The man was bent over, looking at the boy, so you couldn't see his face. The woman was holding the baby and smiling with her cheek pressed against the baby's cheek. The note below the picture said, "Selene, Callum, and Rachel." There was a fourth name before Selene's but it was crossed out so much that there was no trace of what it had said. I picked up the photo to get a closer look.

"That's the only picture we have of both of our parents," a voice said from behind me. I jumped.

"Sorry," Callum smiled. "I didn't mean to startle you."

"No, I'm the one who should be sorry," I interrupted. "I made things awkward because I thought you had a girlfriend. If I had known Selene was your mom-"

"Girlfriend?" He repeated, as he walked towards his room. "Well, that explains some things. That actually would've been terrible of me. No wonder you took off like you did. I wouldn't speak to me ever again either if that was the case. I just don't like to talk about my parents."

He sat down on his bed, rubbing the back of his head nervously. He was obviously upset or embarrassed, or both. I sat down next to him, still holding the photo.

"She's very pretty. You look a lot like her," I said finally.

"She doesn't look like that now," Callum said somberly. "She lives in an assisted living home, bound to a wheelchair and unable to speak or feed herself."

I sat motionless, waiting for Callum to continue.

"Not long after that picture was taken, when I was about two years old, my parents got into a pretty bad fight. My father beat my mother so badly, he almost killed her. He thought he had killed her. Then, he called my grandparents up, told them that Rachel and I'd be goin' to stay with them, and he hung up without another word...and then, he shot himself in the head."

I put my hand up to my mouth.

"A neighbor heard the gunshot and came over to check on us. If she hadn't, my mom would've died. But they got her to the hospital and did what they could to save her. She didn't die, but the brain damage was so bad that she'll never be her old self again."

A tear ran down Callum's cheek and he quickly wiped it away.

"She was a dancer, ya know?" he smiled. "She was a ballet dancer and I loved watchin' her on stage; or so my grandparents always told me. I don't remember since I was so little. And Rachel was fresh out of the womb when it happened."

"You don't remember anything?" I asked.

"I feel like I remember her always smilin'. And all I remember about my father was this big, dark shadow. He was apparently very controlling; he wouldn't let my mother have friends, wouldn't let anyone over to the house, etc. My mother told my grandmother several times that she wanted to leave him. But she was scared he would hurt her. Or us. So the only parents we've ever known were our grandparents. Every time we've asked about our dad, they both told us never to speak about 'that monster,' but it's hard being a boy growin' up without his dad. And we visit our mother when we can, but it's never easy. She just sits there while we make small talk. Always one-sided conversations."

Callum sighed and shook his head before looking back up at me.

"I really do like you, Abby. You're a good, genuine person, and I think you're beautiful. I'm not asking for a lifetime commitment or even a summer fling. Even if you'll only be my friend, that's enough for me. At least I'll still have you in my life. I just don't want to be alone. I've always felt so alone."

I raised my hand to his face and brushed a piece of hair away. He smiled.

"You're not alone. I'm right here."

The words poured out and before I let him say anything else, I reached in to kiss him. Maybe it wasn't the best moment to kiss someone; after confessing so much trauma. But it felt vulnerable and intimate. His tongue slipped into my mouth and his hand cupped one of my breasts. I let out a soft moan as I pushed my body up against his.

"Callum!" Rachel yelled from the top of the stairs.

We broke away from each other.

"If you don't get your arse up here soon, I'm taking your share of tips for the day!"

Callum leaned in and started kissing me again.

"CALLUM!" Rachel roared.

"Yeah, yeah, be up in a minute!" Callum shouted.

We smiled at each other and started laughing.

"Would you like to come over to my aunt and uncle's house for dinner tonight?" I asked. He hesitated for a moment.

"Sure," he answered, smiling.

"And Rachel could come too."

"Oh, I don't know, Abby. Won't that be a little awkward bringin' two strangers over? Plus, Rachel can be a bit much sometimes."

"I thought it would take a little of the heat off of you if your sister came also. That way I'm not inviting a strange boy over to the house."

Callum didn't say anything.

"Look, if you don't want to bring her to dinner, that's fine. I just didn't want to leave her out, and wanted to make things easier for you." He grabbed my hand and kissed it.

"I appreciate you wantin' to include Rachel. I'll get the address from you and after my shift is over, we'll be there. If Rachel wants to go."

Callum got up, grabbed my hand, and pulled me to my feet.

"So, who all will I be meetin'?" he asked. "Give me the rundown."

"Well, first there's my great aunt and uncle. Aunt Poppy is a little odd, but in a fun way, I suppose. Uncle Charles is usually pretty quiet and keeps to himself. I just found out that they had a daughter who died years ago. Uh, but don't tell Rachel. And maybe don't say anything to my aunt and uncle about it."

"Yeah because the first time I meet someone, I like to mention their dead child. Maybe we can swap family tragedy stories."

"Don't be a smart ass," I smirked.

"Sorry. Go on."

"Then, there's my dad. He's really cool for the most part. He's a good guy, just very passive, especially when it comes to my mom. He kind of lets her run the show. He's an IT guy and his company is letting him work remotely, which is how we get to spend the whole summer here. He's very easy to get along with though."

"Nice," Callum grinned as we headed back upstairs.

"And then, my mom. She's never a really cheerful person. She was going to school to become a teacher when she had us, and then ended up being a stay-at-home-mom instead. She's talked about getting another job, She was really close to her cousin who died so I think that might have something to do with the way she is. She likes to drink...a lot. She's an alcoholic. She's always shut herself off from Jo and me. We're not exactly close."

We came back into the restaurant and found Rachel and Jo talking and laughing. Jo was sitting on one of the bar stools and Rachel was standing close to her, resting both elbows on the table.

"So I'm not allowed to chat, but you are?" Callum asked.

"She bought a soda, so I'm talking with a paying customer," Rachel said matter-of-factly before winking at Jo.

"Well, I tried to pay but you insisted it was on the house," Jo laughed.

"I'm inviting Callum, and Rachel if she'd like, over for dinner tonight," I said.

"Is everyone going to be okay with that?" Jo asked.

"It'll be fine," I assured her.

"People generally tend to like me," Callum beamed, "if that's what you're worried about."

I smiled at him.

"I'm in!" Rachel exclaimed. I noticed a moment of excitement on Jo's face.

"Could I have a piece of paper so I can write down the address?" I asked.

Rachel grabbed a tiny notebook and pen from her apron and handed them to me. I flipped past pages of food orders and jotted down the address and my phone number.

"Might want to put Jo's number on there too," Rachel said over my shoulder. "You know, so we can reach both of you if needed."

I wrote Jo's phone number down and sat the pen down on the counter.

"We should be done around five," Callum said. "We'll just need to change clothes and then we'll be over."

"Sounds like a plan," I said. "I'll see you later."

He kissed me on the forehead and walked off.

"I guess I was wrong about you," Rachel smirked. "Maybe you're not a tart after all."

I looked at her and smiled.

"I do miss the pink hair however," she winked.

"So I guess I'll see you in a bit too?" Jo asked.

"Definitely," Rachel breathed.

"Alright, well, see you then!" Jo giggled as we headed out.

Once we were outside, I gave Jo a sly look.

"What?" Jo asked, coyly.

"You have a thing for Rachel, don't you?" I asked.

"Abby, don't make it weird."

"I've seriously never seen you look at someone like that!"

"And you have a crush on Callum, big deal."

"I've had crushes before," I said. "But I don't remember you ever having one. I'm excited for you."

"Just don't do anything to draw attention to it tonight," Jo gritted her teeth. "Please."

"Trust me, I'll be too busy being nervous about Callum being there too."

Jo looked at me as we headed back to the house.

"What have we gotten ourselves into?"

8

"We're home!" I called as Jo and I walked in.

"I wish you girls wouldn't wander about on your own so much," Aunt Poppy sighed. "I worry about you."

"They're fine, Poppy," Uncle Charles said from his chair.

"If it's alright with everyone, I've sort of invited a couple of friends over for dinner," I said timidly.

"Who?" Uncle Charles asked.

"Callum and Rachel," I answered.

"Sounds like returning the clothes went well," my mom said as she entered the room. I smiled at her.

"Oh, of course it's alright!" cried Aunt Poppy, clapping her hands together. "The more, the merrier I always say! Oh, Jo, do you want to help me run to the store and prepare everything?"

"Sure," Jo said.

"Who's Callum and Rachel?" my dad asked from the kitchen.

"The brother and sister I met the first night," I explained loudly.

"Oh, the one with the girlfriend?" he called.

"Turns out it was a misunderstanding," I laughed. "No girlfriend."

I heard my dad let out a quiet, "mmm," before going back to whatever he was doing.

"I think I'll do roast chicken, mashed potatoes, rolls, and green beans," Aunt Poppy said, grabbing her purse.

"Oh, we should also do a charcuterie board," Jo suggested.

They walked out the door without so much as a goodbye to everyone. I stood there awkwardly for a moment.

"Well.." I started. "I think I'm going to sit outside for a bit."

"Come back in if you get too hot," my mom said.

"Okay," I replied.

99

I went outside and walked around the garden beds, reading the little signs for each thing that was growing. Carrots, potatoes, peas, green beans, lettuce, cucumber, tomatoes, strawberries, blueberries, raspberries, watermelon, and several different peppers. There were also two apple trees and a cherry tree. On the other side of the house were rows and rows of herbs. I was so impressed with Aunt Poppy's gardening skills. I made my way over to the tire swing and gave it a tug to see if it was secure. Then I put one foot on the inside of the tire and stood on it. The branch it was hanging from creaked from my weight, but didn't bend. I put both feet through and swung back and forth.

I held onto the tire with both hands as I leaned my head back and kicked my legs out. I closed my eyes as the sunlight sparkled through the leaves.

"Pretty crazy that one day we'll be pushing our kids on this swing, huh?"

I kept my eyes closed as I felt his hands gently push my back.

"I'm just glad my parents are finally letting you come back around the house," I said.

"Probably because I'm leaving soon."

"Please don't remind me. I don't want you to go."

"I know you don't," he said. "Believe me, had I known I was going to be a father soon, I would have never signed up. But it's not forever."

"I just got you back from training. And now you're leaving again. And this time you'll be all the way in Iraq."

"I know," he said, grabbing the swing as it came back towards him. He kissed me on the forehead and breathed against my skin. "But I have to do this. I can't let my family live in a world where people strap bombs to themselves and run into a crowd full of innocent people. I have to do what I can to protect peace and freedom."

"I love you," I said softly as I looked up at him. "You're going to be a great dad."

100

"I love you too. And you're going to be the best mum."

I opened my eyes as I slipped backwards, landing on my back. The tire swing went back and forth above me like a pendulum. I rolled out from underneath it and stood up, holding onto the tree. As I circled around the trunk, my hand ran along the rough bark but stopped when I saw a figure in the treeline of the woods. I squinted, trying to see who it was.

"Olivia?" I asked softly.

I turned to look back at the house and bit my lip. The time on my phone said that it was already 5:03. Callum and Rachel were off of work and would be at the house soon.

"I can make it quick," I muttered as I started towards the woods.

"Abby!" my mom called from the front door. I turned around again. "Aunt Poppy needs help with the green beans. Will you help me pick and trim them?"

I glanced back at the forest. The figure was no longer there. I reluctantly walked back up towards the garden where my mom was holding a large bowl. She showed me how to tell which green beans could be picked and how to take them off without breaking them.

"I didn't know you knew anything about gardening," I said as we picked more green beans.

"My mom...she liked to garden," she said quietly.

"Why don't you ever talk about her?" I asked.

My mom sat back on the dirt and sighed, wiping her sweaty forehead.

"When I found out I was going to be your mom, your grandma promised she'd teach me everything about how to be a mother. She was a great mother herself, very free-spirited and fun. She was the type of mom who let you play hooky from school. Or would make you hot chocolate with extra marshmallows after playing in the snow. She was a single mom so she felt like my best friend more than my mom. I could talk to her about anything. And we were so connected that we could always tell when the

101

other one had something serious going on, before we even told each other."

My mom's eyes filled with tears.

"You and Joanna were toddlers when she died. She saw a couple stranded on the side of the road. They flagged her down and she stopped. As soon as she got close to their car, the man pulled out a gun and shot her. They took off with her car and purse, and left her on the side of the road. She was always so trusting of people. Even after what happened to Olivia."

My mom wiped her cheeks, leaving streaks of dirt on them. I leaned over and wiped the dirt off.

"I'm so...so sorry I've been such a shitty mom to you two. I lost Olivia and then my mom...I fell apart and never put myself back together. And it's incredibly unfair to you girls."

I stared at the bowl of green beans, unable to look her in the eye. I knew I'd cry if I did.

"I haven't drank since we've been here," Mom admitted. "And my goal is to stop completely. Aunt Poppy's been giving me medicine to help me stop."

"Medicine?" I asked.

"A home remedy more or less. I started drinking to numb myself from the pain of losing your grandma and Olivia. I cut off Aunt Poppy for years because I couldn't bring myself to talk to the only other connection I had to the people I lost. But it wasn't fair to her or to you girls to keep you from each other. I've made so many mistakes, and I have *so* many regrets. But I want you to know something."

My mom took my hand in hers and squeezed it.

"You and your sister were never a mistake or a regret. Being your mom is the best thing about me. And I'm really sorry that my grief got in the way of so many years of memories."

I gave my mom the biggest hug I had given her in years. We sat there, in the garden, embracing each other, and crying. Jo poked her head out of the back door.

"Are you guys going to bring those in, or what?"

She stared at us, shocked. My mom motioned for her to come over. Jo hesitantly walked over to us and I grabbed her hand, pulling her down. We hugged her until she finally put her arms around us. Then, I felt another pair of arms in the hug.

"There," Aunt Poppy said gently. "Now my girls can start to heal."

We sat there for a couple more minutes until I heard the sound of two motorcycles getting closer.

"Oh no!" I gasped. "Callum and Rachel!"

"Quick!" Aunt Poppy chirped. "You girls get inside and wash up. We'll finish with the green beans!"

Jo and I ran into the house and upstairs. She refreshed her deodorant and blotted her shiny face with a square of toilet paper. I touched up my makeup and brushed my hair. We ran back down the stairs just as Uncle Charles was answering the door. Callum had on a dark blue polo and khaki shorts, giving him a private school uniform look. Rachel was wearing a long denim skirt, her black chunky boots, and a dark red velvet blouse. The four of us saw each other at the same time and all smiled.

"Well, come on in," Uncle Charles said, moving to the side. "Make yourselves at home."

I greeted Callum with a hug and ushered him into the living room while Rachel and Jo talked quietly to each other. My dad was sitting on the couch, staring at Callum intensely.

"Dad, this is Callum. Callum, this is my dad, Dan."

"Nice to meet you, Dan," Callum said, holding his hand out.

My dad didn't move at first, but after I bugged my eyes out at him, he slowly extended his arm out. Callum twitched slightly and pulled away.

"Quite the grip you have, Dan," he laughed awkwardly.

"Green beans shouldn't take too long!" Aunt Poppy announced as she walked in.

"Pleasure to meet you, Callum," she said as she hugged him.

"Nice to meet you too," Callum chuckled. "This is my sister, Rachel."

Aunt Poppy hugged Rachel too, which made Jo laugh.

"Joanna, why don't you give Rachel and Callum a tour of the house. Abigail, you can set the table."

I blushed at the sound of my full name. I gave Callum an apologetic look and rushed to the kitchen.

"Abby, he's a total dish!" Aunt Poppy giggled as she followed behind me. "And he smells wonderful."

"Ugh, I wanna see him!" my mom complained.

"We need to finish up the food first," Aunt Poppy hissed.

I quickly brought the plates into the dining room and started putting everything in its place.

"Here, let me help," Uncle Charles said, coming up behind me. "I'll finish up here. Go find your sister and your friends."

"Thank you!" I said as I hurried out of the room. I found the three of them upstairs in the hallway. Callum smiled as soon as he saw me.

"Is that one yours?" he asked, pointing to my room. I nodded.

"Wanna see?" I asked.

"Sure."

I flicked on the light switch and held out my arms as if to say, "ta da!" Callum walked around a bit. He pointed at the clock.

"Don't ask," I chuckled.

"You play guitar?"

"Yeah," I said modestly. "I'm not that good though. I can't read music. I just hear something and practice until I copy it."

"That's more than what I can do," Callum said. "I don't have a musical bone in my body. You should hear me sing. Just awful. Like two cats gettin' into a fight."

"I'm sure it's not that bad," I giggled.

"What's this?" he asked, pointing to my sketchbook.

"Oh, nothing. Just something to help me keep track."

"Keep track of what?" He asked, bending down to pick it up.

"You would think I was crazy if I told you."

"Try me."

I let him look through the pages while I told them about my visions and Olivia. After I finished explaining, I waited for him to say something. Anything. Instead he shook his head.

"I told you you'd think I was crazy."

"Abby, don't you realize?"

"What?" I asked.

"Olivia *is* Olivia," he said. "The girl in the woods, the visions, the bathroom cabinets, everythin'. You're in contact with a ghost."

"There's no way Olivia in the woods is the same ghost," I explained. "She looks very much alive. Plus, why would she be haunting me? She died before I was born. She doesn't even know me."

"But your mom was her cousin and her best friend. She can probably sense the close relationship and I think she wants you to find out what happened to her."

"Well, there's one more thing I haven't told you."

"What?" Callum asked.

"I think she showed me another ghost."

"What do you mean?"

"We saw a man in the woods named Seamus Harvey. Olivia acted absolutely terrified of him. And I think he's the same man in my visions. But Uncle Charles said he died shortly after Olivia did. And he was actually a suspect in Olivia's case, but they never found any evidence."

Callum froze with shock.

"What's wrong?" I asked.

"England is one of the most haunted places in the world," Callum laughed nervously. "Every ghost has a story to tell. That's why they get stuck here. Most of the time it's by an unexpected death or a cruel death. They don't know why they're stuck so they have someone else, someone livin', to help them solve it."

"So what should I do?" I asked.

"Find out what happened to Olivia."

"Great. So you're telling me that my dead cousin wants me to figure out how she died?"

"More or less."

I put my head in my hands and groaned.

"I could help you," Callum put his hand on top of my head and played with my hair.

"What immodesty is this?" My aunt yelled in the doorway. "You two shouldn't be up here alone, and on your bed no less!"

"Ma'am, I'm sorry if I disrespected you or Abby in any way," Callum apologized.

"Out! Get out of her room now!"

"Aunt Poppy, it's okay," I begged, completely embarrassed. "We were just talking, that's all."

"Talking can lead to other things, trust me."

"I want you to know that I meant no harm," Callum said. "Really."

Aunt Poppy's face relaxed.

"Just don't let it happen again. Both of you come downstairs now. Dinner is ready."

As we came out of my room, Rachel and Jo came out of the other bedroom, looking a little more disheveled than before. I raised my eyebrows at Jo and her face turned a deep red. When we got to the dining room, everyone else was already seated. Originally, Aunt Poppy had us seated to where Jo was on one side of me and Callum on the other, with Rachel on the other side of him. But I sat in Callum's seat so Jo could sit next to Rachel. Dinner was delicious and we all talked the entire time, including my dad, who started warming up to Callum by the end of the meal.

When it was time to say goodbye, Aunt Poppy put leftovers in containers for Callum and Rachel to take home. They thanked her, then Jo and I walked them out to their bikes. The night air was cool so I wrapped my arms around myself.

"So, where do we start?" Callum asked.

"You really want to help me with this?" I smiled.

"Of course I do. This is all very fascinatin'. I'll go with you tomorrow to the woods. We'll look around a bit and then we'll come back here to the house and look around. See what we see, I suppose."

He nudged me slightly in my arm with his elbow.

"What do you say? Care for an adventure?"

"Sure," I smirked at him.

I gave Callum a goodbye kiss on the cheek while Jo and Rachel sheepishly said goodbye to each other. I watched them get on their bikes and waited until they were out of sight before making our way back to the house.

"We need to talk," I said, locking my arm around my sister's.

"Oh god, Abby. Don't be weird about it. Yeah, we made out. It was amazing. She's definitely as interested as I am, and I'm planning on messaging her as soon as I get upstairs."

"That's actually not what I was talking about," I said. "But I'm happy for you nonetheless."

"Oh."

Everyone was sitting around the living room, drinking tea.

"We're heading to bed!" I announced.

"This early?" my mom asked suspiciously.

"Well, we'll probably have a little bit of girl talk first."

"Can I join?" she asked.

"No," we both said sharply. Mom looked hurt.

"I mean," I laughed, "we're probably going to sleep real soon. Catch you next time though, okay?"

"Sure," my mom mumbled. "Next time."

We went upstairs and I shut the door to my room. I hopped on my bed and bent over the side to get my journal. There, laying next to my dream journal, was the yearbook I had looked at before. It was open. I leaned over to pick it up and look at the page it was opened to. There were rows of faces looking up at me. I noticed that it was open to the "M" names and looked for Murray. There she was. My cousin, the ghost. She graduated in 2007, the year I was born. She was so beautiful and so young.

"Okay," Jo sighed. "What's this all about? You're being extra weird."

"Trust me, this is a big deal. Just hold on a minute."

I continued to look through the yearbook. In the back were pictures of the different school clubs. Something caught my eye and I read the page.

Although fashion at Duncan High is usually a popular topic of discussion, some students are speaking up about being fashion forward, while also being conscious about the environment.

Senior Olivia Murray says that everything from the furniture in her room to the clothes in her closet are second hand.

"I buy everything from either thrift stores or garage sales," Murray said. "I have a waterbed, a shag rug, and I just purchased a vintage grandfather clock. It doesn't work but I'm hoping to find someone who can repair it for a decent price."

When asked about fashion, Murray said her favorite are hats.

"I think hats are fabulous!" Murray said. "You can never go wrong with a good hat. And they can really make an outfit."

With an interest in fashion and a quirky artistic sense, Murray and a few classmates have started their own fashion line that has reached as far as outside London, taking used clothing and refurbishing them into something new.

Murray says she hopes this is only the beginning for her fashion career, however, does not want to get her hopes up.

"Of course every fashion designer hopes to make it big eventually," Murray said. "But my main goal isn't to become famous or anything. I just want people to know that good clothes are out there for a fraction of the cost you can find under big name brands."

You know how the saying goes; "One man's trash is another man's treasure."

When I had finished the article, I looked at the picture next to the column. It was of Olivia, wearing a beret, go-go boots, and a dress with a long-sleeved turtleneck underneath. I thought about the hat boxes under my bed.

"So they were hers," I said aloud to myself.

"Huh?" Jo asked.

"Read this," I said, handing her the yearbook.

Jo read the article and I sat there, patiently waiting for her to finish.

"Okay?" Jo said, sounding annoyed. "It's clearly Aunt Poppy and Uncle Charles' daughter."

"It's the girl I met in the woods. The one I see in my visions!"

"Who?"

"O-liv-i-a Mur-ray. She wants me to help her."

Jo continued to stare at the picture for a while and then slowly closed the yearbook.

"Say it *is* her ghost, and that's why you're having these freaky...visions. Why would she want your help? Why not haunt Mom, or her own parents?"

"I don't know," I sighed. "Maybe she's tried and they won't listen, or maybe because I'm around her age. I don't know! All I know is that she *is* a ghost and she's trying to tell me something about her death! Callum is going to help, but I would rather you be there too. Maybe if she sees another relative, she'll talk to you too. She did mention bringing you the next time I saw her."

Jo stared at me. Her eyes softened and her face relaxed.

"You're my sister, Abby, and more importantly, my twin. Whenever you have a strong emotion I can feel it somehow. I could be miles away with my friends and feel sad all of a sudden, then come home and find out Mom had gotten onto you about something. I know whatever you're going through, whether you're scared, sad, mad, or whatever, I can feel it too. I can tell you've been going through some stuff since we came here because I haven't been sleeping very well. I'll help you as much as I can."

"Thank you, Jo. It means a lot. I hope I can figure things out. For Olivia, Mom, Aunt Poppy, and Uncle Charles."

"So what are the plans?" asked my sister.

"Tomorrow, Callum and I are going down to the woods to try and contact Olivia. Are you in?"

"How long will you be gone?" she asked.

"I don't know. However long it takes."

"Okay, we'll go to the woods tomorrow. And look for our dead cousin's ghost. Totally normal afternoon."

"Let's try and get some sleep," I laughed.

Jo nodded and yawned, causing me to yawn also.

"Goodnight, Abby."

"Goodnight, Jo."

I fell asleep quickly and slept straight through the night. When I opened my eyes, Jo was standing over me.

"Oh, good. You're up. Callum is here. Aunt Poppy has been driving the poor guy nuts."

"Ugh," I moaned. "What time is it?"

"10:00."

"Are you serious?" I said, getting up quickly. "Why didn't you wake me up sooner?"

"I haven't been up that much longer than you. I was taking a bath and heard Callum's voice so I thought I'd come get you."

I rushed to put shorts and a t-shirt on, and then reached for my sketchbook. It wasn't under my bed. I looked around on the floor.

"Did you take my journal?" I asked.

"No. You mean you don't have it?"

Panic swept through me as I searched everywhere.

"No! It's not where I left it! It's not in my room at all!"

"Oh crap. Do you think someone took it?"

"Like who? Olivia?" I asked sarcastically.

"Can ghosts pick things up?"

"I don't know, Jo!"

"Okay, okay. Don't panic. We'll look for it when we get back."

"If Mom finds that, she's going to lose it."

I put a pair of tennis shoes on and the two of us went downstairs.

"There's the sleeping beauty!"

"Good morning, Aunt Poppy," I muttered as Jo snuck off into the kitchen.

"You've been keeping this poor boy waiting for a while. He said you two have a picnic planned!"

"Uh, yeah," I eyed him. "A picnic."

"Alright. Just promise you're not getting on that death trap of his."

"Huh?" I asked.

"My bike," Callum snickered. "And no, we'll be walking from here."

I nodded in agreement.

"Good!" Aunt Poppy sighed. "Alright well you kids have fun!"

"Thanks!" I said as she went into the kitchen.

"Sorry I kept you waiting," I said before giving Callum a kiss on the cheek. "How long have you been here?"

"Not very long. Only fifteen minutes or so."

"In this house? That's a long time."

"Well if you give me another kiss, I'll completely forgive you," he winked.

I giggled and gave him another kiss. He pulled away as Jo came up from behind me and waved hello.

"Oh, Jo's coming with us too," I smiled. Callum's expression changed.

"Oh, okay."

"I don't have to if it's going to interfere with anything," Jo said.

"No, it's totally fine," Callum grinned. "The more, the merrier!"

"I brought some snacks," Jo said, holding a bag up. "Mostly cookies and apples."

"Alright, well, let's get going," I said.

We walked outside and Callum pulled his phone out quickly.

"Shit," Callum groaned.

111

"What's wrong?" I asked.

"Someone didn't show up for their shift. I have to go to work."

"Seriously?"

"I know," he sighed. "I'm so sorry. I'll message you after I get off to see how the ghost hunting goes."

"Okay," I said as he quickly kissed my forehead.

I watched as Callum quickly got on his motorcycle without looking back at me, and sped off.

"Oh man," Jo said. "I'm so sorry. He left because of me, didn't he?"

"I...I don't know," I mumbled. "That was kind of odd."

"You can message him that I decided not to go and see if he comes back."

"If he left because of you, he can go," I stated. "You're my sister. Besides, I'm not pushing you away anymore. We're in this together."

I started down the road and Jo followed after me. While we walked towards the woods, we talked about school and our friends.

"She still hasn't messaged you back?" Jo asked when I mentioned Sarah.

"Nope," I sighed. "I don't know what her deal is. I think I might have pushed her away."

"What makes you say that?"

"I'm not a pleasant person, Jo," I scoffed. "I don't know if I'd want to be friends with myself. I don't like who I'm becoming."

"Abby, you've always been hard on yourself. You're smart, you're charming, you're funny, and you're very pretty! I've always been envious of how carefree you are. You don't go out of your way to impress anyone. You don't care what anyone thinks."

"Maybe that's the problem," I contemplated "Maybe I should start caring a tiny bit."

"Maybe I should start caring a bit less," Jo said.

"You really think I'm smart?" I smiled at her.

"Well, yes. Not as smart as me. But you're a clever girl. And wisdom doesn't always necessarily mean intelligence."

"Thanks...I think."

As we approached the stream, we slowed down to look around. Jo saw the initials carved in the huge rock.

"Mom," she said as she traced our mother's initials.

"This is the spot where I first saw her," I said.

"Hm, maybe she's not here," suggested Jo.

"Olivia!" I called out. The sudden noise startled Jo, along with two large, gray squirrels, who ran up a tree when I shouted. Jo grabbed her chest.

"Sorry," I said.

"Do you think it's because I'm here?" she asked.

"I wouldn't think so. She told me to bring you."

I leaned on the carved rock and crossed my arms, thinking. Jo came over and sat down next to me.

"It's beautiful out here," Jo sighed. "A little creepy. But beautiful."

"Abby, is that you?"

Jo and I turned towards the voice. Olivia was standing a few feet away from us by a tree. Jo and I jumped to our feet, shocked to see her.

"Olivia!" I exclaimed. "You're here."

"Yes, of course I am. I told you, this is basically all I do every day."

She looked at Jo.

"Who's this?" She blinked.

"This is Jo," I said, gently pushing my sister forward.

"Hi," Jo waved awkwardly.

"Joanna," Olivia waved back. "My name is Olivia. It's so nice to meet you."

"Yeah, you too."

I nudged Jo with my elbow. She was being obviously creeped out. Olivia walked slowly towards us. I never noticed how she always seemed to glide as she walked, almost like she was floating above the ground. Jo and I backed away from her. She stopped.

"What's the matter? You're acting as if you're afraid of me."

Neither of us said anything and Olivia frowned.

"What's going on, Abby?"

"Listen," I started. "I don't know how to tell you this...because you might not be aware of it..."

"What?" Olivia asked.

"You're dead, Olivia."

She blinked.

"I've seen visions of how you died and I saw your yearbook. You're not eighteen; you were 18 in 2007. You were really into fashion and liked buying everything secondhand, including the furniture in your bedroom. And for some reason the smell of bergamot reminds your parents, my great-aunt and uncle, of you. And I think Seamus Harvey killed you. But I need you to help me so I can help you."

When I finished, I let out a long sigh, trying to catch my breath. Finally, Olivia spoke.

"I've been in that house so many times, trying to talk to my parents. But they ignore me, which is strange because my mother used to try so hard to communicate with me. I'm sorry if I've scared you, I just didn't know what to do."

Olivia smiled weakly at us.

"Did you say you've been having visions?" she asked. I nodded.

"It's like I'm you every time, reliving what you went through. And I'm able to draw out the scene with details."

"Your sketchbook you showed me," she said.

"It's really bizarre to watch it happen to her," Jo added. "Her eyes roll back and sometimes she mumbles."

"Do you not have the gift?" Olivia asked.

"No, thank goodness," Jo scoffed. "Sometimes my stomach hurts randomly right before something happens. But that could just be IBS."

"Don't feel bad for Jo," I swatted playfully. "She's gifted in other ways. She's really smart, especially with science and math. And she's a great cook."

"A kitchen witch," Olivia whispered.

"Huh?" Jo asked.

"Olivia, did you take my sketchbook?" I inquired.

"No, of course not," she replied. "Why?"

"I guess I've misplaced it. And it has all of my drawings from my...visions. I feel so silly calling them that."

"Don't feel silly," Olivia giggled. "A lot of witches have some degree of divination powers, but yours seem quite powerful. Embrace your natural gifts The Goddess has bestowed upon you."

"Witches?" Jo crossed her arms. "Goddess? Gifts? You can't be serious."

"Your grandma was an Irish witch, wasn't she?" I asked.

"She taught us everything we know," Olivia beamed. "Gardening, medicine, meditation, astrology, divination...although I was never that great at divination. I was always more in tune with nature. Will used to say I was like a fairytale princess because all sorts of woodland creatures would approach me. They weren't scared of me at all. I guess that's why I'm stuck here."

"I want to help you, Olivia. I want you to be able to move on, but I don't know how. And Seamus Harvey died already, didn't he? So there's no way we could have the police arrest him."

"But no one knows where my body is!" cried Olivia.

"Do you?" Jo asked.

Olivia looked around before shaking her head.

"I only remember bits and pieces."

"We'll help you," I said. "But you have to give us something to start with."

Olivia pondered a moment.

"My parents used to keep stuff in the attic. Important stuff. Maybe you'll find something up there."

"Okay," I said. "Jo and I will start in the attic and see what we can find."

"Okay, well then I guess we're off to look in the attic," Jo said. "And we'll report back here at this exact same spot."

"Thank you," Olivia smiled. "Oh, and Abby? Please don't say anything. I don't want this upsetting anyone."

I nodded and smiled. Suddenly, Olivia disappeared from sight. It was only Jo and me standing in the forest.

"I can't believe that just happened," I whispered.

"Neither can I."

Thunder roared above us and we both jumped.

"We better get back before it starts pouring down," I suggested.

We walked as fast as we could, however, about halfway to the house the rain started coming down hard. Neither of us had an umbrella nor jacket, so we ran. We got up to the house and I stopped to look back at the woods. I thought I saw something- or *someone*- move at the edge of the forest. We got inside the door. The house was quiet.

9

"Hello?" I called out.

My phone started vibrating in my pocket. I pulled it out at the same time Jo did. We had several missed text messages from Mom and Dad saying that they had gone out with Aunt Poppy and Uncle Charles to buy some supplies to renovate the house. I quickly messaged her back saying that I had lost service and that Jo and I were at the house.

"How much time do you think we have?" Jo asked, her wet hair dripping.

"Hopefully long enough to find what we're looking for," I sighed.

Jo and I walked up the stairs and looked up at the door that led to the attic.

"I'll get a chair," Jo said before walking away.

I stepped into my room to search for my sketchbook again. I looked everywhere and couldn't find it.

"Still not there?" Jo asked from the doorway, holding one of the dining room chairs.

"Nope," I sighed. "I don't understand how it just disappeared."

"Hold on," Jo said, setting the chair down and walking away. She returned a minute later with a coloring book and a box of crayons.

"These have been in my room," she said, handing them to me. "It's the best I can do until we find your journal or get you a new one."

"Thanks," I smirked. "To the attic?"

"To the attic," Jo repeated.

She climbed up on the chair and pulled the chain that hung from the door in the ceiling.

"Back up," Jo called down to me. I took a step back as she pulled down. A small ladder appeared as the door opened. Jo pulled down on the ladder and it extended down to the hallway floor.

"After you," Jo said, gesturing up.

"Gee, thanks."

I carefully climbed the rickety ladder up to the attic. The room was packed full of boxes and piles of assorted things. There were paintings and framed photographs. There was an old rocking horse and a little red wagon. Next to those, there was a box of dress-up clothes and a wooden kitchen set. I bent down and ran my fingers across the carved stove top.

"Oh my god," Jo said as she came up. "There's so much shit up here."

We took our phones out and turned the flashlights on. I looked through a box of glass dolls. Some were tattered and filthy, but some were in good shape. I took out one, who was wearing a yellow dress and ran my fingers through her hair. Her painted brown eyes looked up at me.

"Creepy," Jo whispered. "I hate old dolls like that."

I sat the doll carefully back down into the box and stood up.

"I don't know what I'm supposed to be looking for," I sighed.

"Here's a bunch of photographs," Jo said, looking into a large cardboard box.

The two of us went through each one. A lot of the pictures were of people I didn't know, although I figured they were relatives that had passed away. I came across a wedding picture from a long time ago. Although the faces had changed, the smiles had not.

"Is that Aunt Poppy and Uncle Charles?" Jo asked. I nodded.

Aunt Poppy was very pretty, but looked very young, close to my age. She had a small, round face with a hint of blush in her cheeks. Her hair was dark and was up off of her shoulders. Uncle Charles looked tall and proud next to his bride. While Aunt Poppy was looking at the camera in the picture, Uncle Charles was looking at her.

"I want this," I smiled.

"Well since it's up here, I don't think they would mind you taking it. At least someone would be enjoying it."

"I meant I want *this*. I want someone looking at me when I look at the camera. I want fifty years or more with the same person. I want someone to be by my side and tell me everything is going to be okay."

I went back to looking through the pictures, not saying anything. Nothing important was found so we moved on. I looked through some of the paintings. Nothing. Under one of the paintings I found a pile of fashion books.

"These must have been Olivia's. No one else in the house was interested in fashion."

Laying next to the books was a box of odds and ends. A couple of tennis trophies, some paintbrushes, tubes of lipstick, and a key. The key caught my eye. I picked it up and examined it. At the top of the key there was a small design carved into it. It was a tree.

"Jo, I think I know what this goes to!" I said excitedly.

Without waiting for her to reply, I quickly made my way back down to my room, opened the grandfather clock to take out the box and ran over to my bed with it. I wiped the sweat off of my forehead and slowly put the key into the lock. I turned it carefully until I heard a click. I took off the lock and opened the box. The box seemed to be filled with papers. As I reached for the piece of paper on the top, Jo rushed into the room.

"They're back," she said, panicking. "I just heard the car pull up."

"I'll go help them bring stuff from the car and you get everything put back!" I said, running out of my room and around the ladder. I stubbed my toe on the chair hard and tripped.

"Ow, shit!" I yelled as I hopped on one foot towards the stairs.

"Jesus, Abby, are you serious?" Jo yelled as she started pushing the ladder back up. "Pull yourself together!"

I ran out to the car in the rain as Aunt Poppy popped open her umbrella.

"Abigail?" she squinted at me. "Get back inside, you'll catch your death out here!"

"I'm fine," I said quickly. "Just wanted to come help!"

I ran around to the other side and helped Uncle Charles get out of the back seat. I held onto his arm as he stood up slowly with his cane.

"Thanks, Olivia."

Our wide eyes met each other and then quickly turned away.

"I- I'm so sorry, Abby," he apologized.

"It's okay," I smiled wearily. "Mom calls me and Jo each other's names and we don't look anything alike."

"You're a sweet girl, you know that?"

Uncle Charles patted my shoulder and made his way towards the house, sharing the umbrella with Aunt Poppy. Luckily, they were moving a little slow so I turned my attention to my parents, who were unloading the trunk.

"What all did you buy?" I asked as I grabbed bags.

"I'm going to put in all new light fixtures," my dad explained, grabbing a few boxes. "I need to paint the kitchen cabinets, take out the old linoleum floor, and put in new flooring. And there's a spot on the roof that got hit by a large tree branch. I need to patch it before it starts leaking."

"Why don't they just move to a newer house?" I grunted as I carried the bags in. "They don't even use the upstairs.

"This house holds a lot of special memories," my mom said solemnly. "It holds a lot of magic."

"Witches," I muttered.

"What?" Mom asked.

"Nothing."

We walked inside and Jo was sitting on the couch, reading a book. She looked up at me and winked.

"Couldn't be bothered to help the rest of us, huh?" Dad said as he sat the boxes on the coffee table.

"Sorry, I've been catching up on..." she looked at the cover of the book she was holding. "...the Irish Republican Army."

"When you're finished, let me know what you think!" Uncle Charles exclaimed as he took his usual seat.

"I'm actually going to put this in my room," Jo smiled. "Abby, would you help me?"

"Take a book upstairs?" I asked.

Jo's eyes widened and she gave me a pleading look. Once we were in her room, she shut the door and tossed the book on her bed.

"Get this. I was looking through cookbooks in the living room, so I could get some ideas on meals I want to try making. I picked up one and opened it. Abby, this one wasn't a cookbook. A lot of them aren't. Someone took cookbook sleeves and put them over the actual books so no one would see what kind of books they really are."

"What kind of books are they?" I asked.

"Ghost books."

"What?"

"Pagan books on how to communicate with the dead. Breaking through 'the veil,' as they call it."

"Do you think that's how Olivia is here?" I asked. "Aunt Poppy did something from one of those books and it somehow summoned Olivia's spirit?"

"I don't know," Jo shook her head. "But I was thinking, if the books *are* right, and you *can* summon a spirit, what if we summon Seamus Harvey?"

10

Dinner went on without anyone saying much. I shoveled food into my mouth as quickly as possible. Uncle Charles kept side-eyeing me, but no one else seemed to notice. I cleaned my plate and made my way towards the stairs.

"Abigail, where are you going?" asked Aunt Poppy.

"To bed," I said quickly.

"This early?"

"I don't feel so well," I lied.

"Probably ate too fast," Uncle Charles stated.

"I'm also just really tired," I added.

"I'd really like us all to sit down and talk about something," Aunt Poppy said.

"I'm really tired too," Jo said, standing up quickly to take her plate to the sink.

"What has gotten into you two?" Aunt Poppy asked. "I really think we should-"

"Aunt Poppy," Mom said, "just let them go. It can wait."

There was an awkward pause as Jo rinsed her plate. Once she was finished, I smiled at everyone.

"Well, goodnight then," I announced.

"Night," Jo chimed in.

Everyone told us goodnight and we ran up the stairs.

"Grab the box and meet me in my room," Jo whispered.

I retrieved the box from my room and quickly rushed in to dump its contents on Jo's bed. She shut the door and pulled three books out from under her bed.

"Are those the ones you were talking about?" I asked. Jo nodded and started looking through them as I inspected what had been inside the locked box. There were a couple of small pictures and a few written letters. I picked up one letter and read it:

Liv,

It was so good hearing back from you so soon! I know we talk on the phone a lot but I'm always so excited to get letters from you. Sorry I haven't been able to talk to you as often. College is kicking my ass. You didn't sound as though you had just had two babies! I'm really proud of you Liv. I'm glad you kept them. I know you're only two years younger than me but you just seem like you've grown up so much. I guess motherhood will do that to you! I can't wait to see them this summer. We'll go out and get clothes for the twins and just spoil them rotten! I was wondering if you had heard anything from Will yet, or whether or not his mom was getting any better about the whole situation. I know you said his dad had come up to the hospital, so that's good. At least one of them is being supportive. And I'm sure his mom will come around. Does Will know yet that he's officially a dad?

I still haven't heard from my dad. I guess he doesn't need a daughter now that he has a son and a new wife. But I think I'm becoming okay with that. Like you said, he's the one missing out. And I have to act like it doesn't bother me or else my mom gets upset. I wish she wanted to move back to England. I would in a heartbeat. I wish I could go to school out there. I just can't bring myself to leave Mom all alone. Can't wait to hear from you, and send a picture of you and the twins in your next letter. I want one to hang up in my dorm.

Love you lots, Maggie

P.S.- Never forget, you're not only my cousin, you're my best friend!

I was extremely confused as I read the letter.

"What the-" Jo gasped as she picked up another piece of paper.

"What?" I asked. "What is it?"

"It's your birth certificate."

Jo and I read the paper over and over, neither of us speaking. Jo looked through the papers and found a similar paper.

"Abby, look."

We stared at the papers in silence. I was certain that Jo was reading and re-reading hers, just like I was, trying to make sense of it all.

"Oh my god," I finally said,

I read my first name. Abigail. That was correct. I read my middle name. Poppy. That was also correct. Then, I read my last name. Murray; not Mitchell. And instead of Margaret, the name under the Mother's line read Olivia. It was the same as Jo's birth certificate.

"This is a mistake," Jo said, shaking her head. "It has to be a mistake."

"No, I don't think it is a mistake. Look at this."

I handed the letter to Jo and waited for her to read it as I sat there, shaking.

"How can this be possible?"

"Have you ever seen pictures of Mom pregnant?" I asked quietly.

"That doesn't mean anything. Maybe she just didn't want any pictures of her looking fat. That seems to be pretty on par for her."

"Or maybe because she never was pregnant, Jo!"

"But I look like Dad. Everyone says so."

"Maybe because we don't know what our real dad looks like. You could look a lot like him."

"No, our parents are Maggie and Dan."

"Jo! These papers say Olivia. Not Margaret."

"I don't believe it."

"Well there's one way to find out."

I grabbed the two birth certificates and ran downstairs. Jo ran after me. Aunt Poppy, Uncle Charles, and my...mom were sitting in the living room. Aunt Poppy stopped talking as soon as she saw us.

"I thought you two went to bed," Aunt Poppy said before taking a sip of tea.

"What the hell are these?" I held out the papers to my mom. As she registered what they were, her eyes widened.

"What are they?" Uncle Charles asked her.

"Abigail's and Joanna's birth certificates," she said softly. The cup in Aunt Poppy's hand slipped and crashed to the floor.

"So it's true?" I yelled. "You're not our mom?"

"Honey, I've wanted to tell you two since you arrived," Aunt Poppy cried.

"What's going on in here?" my dad asked, sprinting into the room.

I glared at him.

"Of all people, I thought I could trust you. And you never said anything! You kept it a secret for *her*!"

He stood there in silence.

I looked over at Maggie, my *cousin*.

"And you!" I pointed a finger at her. "You've treated us like crap, especially me. How could you?"

"Honey, we wanted to tell you two," started Dan.

"We just didn't know how," added Maggie.

"SHUT UP!" I screamed at her. At this point almost everyone in the room was crying.

"I think we all need to calm down," Uncle Charles suggested.

"You never tried to tell us anything," Jo said with a quiet, shaky voice. "You made us think we weren't liked by our own parents."

"Jo, we love you two very much," Dan's voice cracked.

"You never wanted us, did you?" I asked, voice trembling. "You were just doing our real mom a favor."

"She didn't have to take you two," Poppy sobbed. "We could've taken you. She offered to take care of you because she thought it's what your mom would have wanted."

"It's a shame she did such a bad job at it," I said sharply.

"Abby, please," Maggie stepped towards me. I backed away. "I thought I could take care of you. I was only twenty years old. I was engaged at the time and going to college. I really thought I could do it all. My mom was willing to help and loved you two because you reminded her of her and Poppy."

Aunt Poppy wiped her cheeks.

"But after my mom died, I felt so lost," she continued. "Dan and I did our best but we were in over our heads taking care of two infants. We lived in a one bedroom apartment and I had to drop out of college. I got a job at a daycare so I could get discounted childcare while Dan finished school. Luckily he found a job that supported us enough that I could stay home with you two until you started school. But by then I was depressed and..."

Maggie started crying harder.

"I started drinking a lot. I did it to cope with my grief, and then I did it because I needed it. I did it to self-medicate. And I really did lose myself in the process. I wanted to be like my mother, and I'm sorry I wasn't. I'm sorry for everything."

"You're sorry?" I scoffed. "You've hit me. You've called me a bitch. You made me feel like I was the biggest inconvenience. You do realize how much therapy Jo and I are going to need because of you. You should be sorry. Sorry for never accepting me for who I am. Sorry for never being there when I needed a mother. Sorry for walling yourself off to the children you promised you'd take care of. SORRY FOR NEVER TELLING ME YOU'RE NOT MY FUCKING MOTHER!"

"Abby, can you please just calm down?" she asked. "I'm willing to talk now. I'll answer any questions you girls have."

"Talk? Why would I listen to anything you have to say? Why would I trust anything you say when all you've ever done is lie to me?"

"Okay, you can talk and I'll listen."

"I don't have anything to say to you people. I hate all of you."

I ran to the door to leave, but my dad- or my uncle- grabbed my arm.

"No, Abby. You're not running again."

"Let go of me, *Dan!*"

"No, Abby!"

Without thinking, I turned around and punched him in the face. Pain shot through my knuckles, into my hands, and up my arm. I had never hit anyone before, and I was pretty sure I broke something. He let out a howl of pain and let go of me. As he reached up to hold his face, I ran out the door and away from the house. I didn't stop running until I saw Trotter's. I reached the door but it was locked. Looking through the glass window, I saw that the back room light was off.

"Callum!" I shouted, banging on the door. "Rachel! Are you there?"

A light in the back turned on and Rachel appeared, coming up to the front door. When she recognized me, she unlocked it and let me in. I pulled my phone out long enough to message Jo that I was safe and then turned it off.

"Abby?" Rachel asked, concerned. "Is everythin' alright?"

"No," I started to cry. "No, it's not alright. Is Callum here?"

"Yeah, he's downstairs. Come on in."

As we walked down the stairs, Rachel called out, "we've got ourselves a visitor, bruv."

Callum came out of his room in plaid pajama pants and a shirt. He saw me, smiled, but the smile quickly faded.

"Abby, what's wrong?"

"She's my mom, Callum."

"Who?"

"Olivia."

Callum looked at Rachel and nodded towards her room.

"Oh, right," she looked around awkwardly before backing into her room. "I'll just be in here..."

"How do you know that?" he asked quietly as soon as Rachel shut the door.

I explained to him about the birth certificates and what happened with my family.

"Oh, Abby, I'm sorry."

"Don't be," I sighed. "I just don't know how to handle all of this. And I feel like Jo and I have to spend the rest of the summer in a house full of strangers."

"Well they're still your parents, sort of, aren't they?"

"How do you figure?" I asked.

"They're still the ones who have taken care of you and raised you all these years," explained Callum. "I know your mom did a shite job but you've always had a nice home, clothes, food, and everythin' else you've ever needed. They didn't have to take you guys, but they did. I consider my grandpa more as a dad than a grandparent."

"But they lied to me and Jo."

"Because they didn't want to hurt you guys," said Callum. "And there's a lot of trauma behind why they ended up havin' to take you in. How would you feel if you were them?"

I thought about it for a moment.

"Look, if you're not ready to go back, you can stay here until you're ready," said Callum. "Rachel!"

Rachel came back in the room with us.

"Do you mind if Abby stays here for a bit?" he asked.

"I wouldn't want to impose," I said quietly.

"Rubbish!" cried Rachel. "Of course you can stay here."

"Um, where am I sleeping?" I asked.

Callum and Rachel looked at each other.

"Oh man, I am tired!" Rachel said before yawning dramatically and making her way to her room. I looked at Callum who smiled at me. A shirt and shorts flew at me from Rachel's room.

"Pajamas for you," she said before shutting her door.

"Oh, thanks!" I called. "Goodnight!"

"Goodnight, kiddies!"

I went into the bathroom to change into the borrowed pajamas.

When I came out of the bathroom, Callum had placed a blanket and pillow on the couch.

"What is that?" I asked.

"My temporary bed."

"No, you can-"

"No," he stopped me. "You have the bed. I'll be fine."

"Are you sure?" I asked.

"Yes, I'm sure," Callum said before kissing me on the cheek. "Goodnight, love."

"Goodnight," I replied.

I started walking to Callum's room and turned around as he was taking his shirt off. He got under the blanket and laid his head down. I stood there, biting my lip, thinking. I really wanted him to sleep with me since I felt a little scared staying in a new place. On the other hand, I didn't want him to get the wrong idea. I was a virgin, and I had only ever kissed two other boys before Callum. One of those was a childhood crush that I kissed on the cheek in third grade. I walked over the couch and stood over him.

"Callum," I said softly. He looked up at me.

"What's wrong?"

I pulled the blanket back a little and took his hand in mine. He stood up, looking puzzled. I wrapped my arms around his neck and hugged him. He put his hands on my waist and put his forehead against mine.

"I don't want to be alone tonight," I whispered.

He gently cupped my bottom with his hands and picked me up as I wrapped my legs around his waist and he carried me to his room. He laid me down on his bed carefully and shut the door.

"Callum?"

"Yeah?"

"I...uh, don't want you to get the wrong idea about me," I gulped. "I, uh, don't want to-"

"We'll go at your pace and you tell me when to stop," he breathed into my ear. I pulled him on top of me and started kissing him.

We ended up doing more than I had originally intended, but we still didn't have sex. I was proud of myself for telling a boy when to stop. Callum seemed a little disappointed, but respected my boundaries regardless. We fell asleep in each other's arms, and for a little while, I was too distracted with my own happiness to think about my family, ghosts, and an unsolved murder.

I woke up the next day feeling refreshed and still tired at the same time. I looked over at Callum, who was still sleeping. He was on his stomach with his arms wrapped around his pillow. His lips were slightly parted, which made me want to kiss them. Instead, I let him continue to sleep and silently snuck out of the room.

"Oh, you're up!"

Rachel and Jo were sitting on the couch.

"Shit," I muttered.

"Oh my god, Abby!" Jo snapped at me. "Your idea of coping with what happened yesterday is losing your virginity to the first guy in Europe who shows interest in you?"

"I didn't lose my virginity," I blushed.

"What were all the noises I heard last night?" Rachel asked, raising her eyebrows.

I paused for a moment.

"Third base," I admitted through gritted teeth.

"Oh gross," Rachel fake-gagged. "I'm going to shower before I have to start work."

She kissed Jo on the cheek and went to the bathroom.

"You promise that's all that happened?" Jo asked. "Our mom was a teen mom. I don't want this to be a hereditary thing."

"Yes, Jo," I rolled my eyes.

"Good."

"Wait," I said. "What are you even doing here?"

"Well, you left and everyone got worried. I got your message and knew where you were. I told everyone that you were staying with Rachel. Left out the part about Callum being here. They asked me to come by and talk to you. They want you to come home."

"That's not home, Jo," I explained. "Besides, I can't be around any of them right now. In a matter of days, we found out that our parents aren't our real parents, our mom had us at a young age and was murdered when we were still babies, and her ghost is currently haunting that house and the woods behind it. It's too much. I need a break."

"And everyone said they're willing to do that for you," Jo sighed. "But you've got to stop running away every time things get hard. You have to start facing the hard shit so you can learn how to deal with it."

Tears filled my eyes as I sat down on the couch next to Jo. She grabbed my hands and looked into my eyes.

"I don't care that Maggie and Dan aren't our parents. I don't care that we won't ever know our real parents. You're the only constant in my life, and you always have been. You're my sister. My twin. You're my family, forever and ever. I'm always going to be there for you, no matter what. So whenever you feel like running away from everything, at the very least, run to me. Okay?"

I nodded, unable to speak. Jo smiled at me and squeezed my hands.

"Okay then," she breathed. "Do whatever you need to do, check in when you can, and come back soon."

"Okay," I squeaked.

"Promise?" Jo asked.

"I promise. Just let me have the day to myself and then I'll be back."

"By the way," Jo said, "I brought some stuff."

She pulled a backpack out from the other side of the couch and opened it.

"I brought those books I found, the box full of papers, and a notepad and pen, in case you have another vision."

"What are those?" I asked, pointing to multiple pieces of paper sticking out of one of the books.

"I stayed up late last night reading about the veil," Jo said, opening up to a page. "Certain people have personal veils that are thinner than others. Also, the veil is thinner during certain times of the day and year. Dawn, dusk, and the witching hour."

"The witching hour?" I asked.

"Between three and four in the morning," Jo explained. "And then, no surprise here, Samhain is the day of the year when the veil is the thinnest."

I gave her a puzzled look.

"Around Halloween," Jo said sharply. "Also, according to the book, any electronics interfere with breaching the veil. Which is probably why Poppy and Charles don't own a television."

"I don't get it," I shook my head. "If Poppy believes in all of this stuff, and has tried so hard for years to contact her daughter, why hasn't it worked before? Why is it working now?"

"You, Abby. You're obviously the connection to our mom. And I'm betting Poppy knew one of us would be. The first night we were here, I overheard her and Mom- Maggie, talking about how we've been invited here every summer and every Christmas since we've been born. Maggie and Dan didn't think we were old enough until this year. Poppy and Charles have sent us birthday and Christmas money every year and they have a savings account set up for us for college."

"What!" I exclaimed. "Why didn't you say anything before now?"

"I didn't think a whole lot of it," she shrugged. "I just thought they were generous relatives who wanted to do something nice for us. I wouldn't have ever guessed it was because they're our grandparents. But we're here now and you have a chance to do what Poppy never could."

"Yeah," I said, running my fingers across the book's page. "I guess she got what she wanted."

It felt as if my hair was going to rip out of my head as Seamus dragged me deeper and deeper into the woods. Every time I started to scream, Seamus would stop long enough to kick me in the stomach until my screaming stopped, then continued to walk. I knew I had at least one broken rib. I heard it snap and breathing was agonizing. I didn't want to die. Not like this. I had twin babies that I was responsible for. I had a boyfriend that would come back from his deployment soon. I wish I could have

132

held my babies one more time. I started weeping and Seamus tugged on my head.

"Please," I gasped.

"Shut up!" he snarled at me. "This is going to happen no matter what you do so you might as well shut up. The other one was so much easier."

"Other one?" I asked.

"The one you saw me kill. Of course the little ones are always easier. They're so trustworthy."

I'm so scared, I thought. I tried to break free and Seamus grabbed my hand, breaking two of my fingers like they were twigs. I shrieked and another blow to the stomach knocked the wind out of me. I tried hard to stay conscious; to focus on my other senses. What did I smell? The minty yarrow as it brushed my face. What did I taste? Blood. No, don't focus on that. What did I hear? The rain drops hitting the leaves of the sycamore trees. I started getting tunnel vision and knew I was close to passing out. Stop it! Focus on the forest. Focus on the stream. The sound of the rushing water was somehow soothing in the midst of all of this pain and fear. I looked up to the cloudy sky, the soft rain falling down on me. Seamus continued to drag me along the stream until he suddenly threw me down. I didn't try to get up and run because I was so tired and sore, and I knew he could catch me easily.

My head was throbbing and my whole body hurt. I realized I had urinated at some point and the smell combined with my sweat made me nauseous. I threw up bile and moaned as the muscles in my stomach spasmed. Seamus grabbed something from his back pocket and pulled it out. It was rope. He used it to tie my hands together tight.

"You're not going to rape me, are you?" I asked him.

"Ha! You're too old. I like mine younger and untouched. You're eighteen and already have babies. No tellin' how many boys you've let between your legs. You're too filthy for me."

He propped me up on my knees and moved my hair out of my face. He held up the camera around his neck up.

133

"Now, if you would be so kind as to smile for me?"

"Eat shit," I said before I spat in his face.

"Oh, well now. That wasn't very lady-like."

Seamus drew back a fist and punched me in the mouth. It felt like my jaw had shattered into a million pieces. I let out a cry of pain and spat out blood, a few teeth came out as well. Seamus held up the camera again. It clicked and flashed before the film slid out.

"Thank you," he cheerfully said, sitting the camera down on a nearby rock.

"Now then. Let's get this started, shall we?"

He grabbed me by my hair again and suddenly threw me into the stream. I broke the surface gasping for air. Seamus jumped in behind me and I could feel him push my head under the water. I tried to scream but all that came out were bubbles. This was it; the place I would die. But I wasn't ready to leave yet. I held on for as long as I could, thinking about Will, my parents, and Maggie. Thinking about Abigail and Joanna. My beautiful girls. My last thought was that I would do everything in my power to make sure I saw them again...and then, darkness...

Tears streamed down my face as I opened my eyes. Jo, Callum, and Rachel were standing over me and Jo was holding my hand, crying.

"Oh god, Abby," she sobbed. "I saw it. I saw what happened to our mom."

"Y-you did?" I asked. She nodded.

I looked down at the notepad in my lap. The entire page had been filled with the blue ink from the pen.

"What happened?"

"You started drawin' a man," Callum explained with a shaky voice. "He was holdin' somethin' down under water. And then you started fillin' the entire page with scribbles."

Rachel nodded slowly.

"We have to tell someone what we saw," Jo said, standing up.

"Who are we going to tell, Jo?" I asked. "We can't go to the police about a murder that happened when we were babies. They'd think we were insane."

"We can tell our family!"

"We don't know what he did with her body."

I stood up quickly and started packing everything into the backpack.

"I need more answers first," I added. "Go back to the house. Tell everyone that I'm safe and that I'll be back later."

"What are you going to do?" Jo asked.

"I'm going to find out where Seamus Harvey lived and check it out."

"Abby..."

"It'll be fine, Jo. He's dead. He can't hurt anyone anymore. But I'm going to try and contact him and find out what he did with the bodies."

"*Bodies?*" Rachel asked, glancing at Callum.

"He killed at least one other girl that I know of," I said. "But I think there might be more."

"I'm coming with you," Jo said.

"No! I need you to go home and act like everything is perfectly normal. Just hang out at the house until you hear from me. I don't want anyone getting suspicious."

"I'll go with you," Callum said. "I only work a half shift today and then I'll meet up with you."

"There," I smiled at Jo. "I won't be alone. Callum will make sure I stay safe."

Jo looked at us, unsure.

"It'll be fine," I reassured her.

"Okay," Jo said. "Get a hold of me as soon as you find something."

"Promise," I grinned.

"We need to head upstairs," Callum said.

"I should head back to the house," Jo sighed.

We all said our goodbyes and as soon as Jo and I were outside on the sidewalk, we gave each other a big hug before going our separate ways. The weight of my last vision started to fully sink in. I hadn't had the chance to grieve the loss of my loved one. I hadn't even known I had lost a loved one until last night. My mom died shortly after I was born; she was killed. She hadn't done anything to deserve it either. As I followed the sidewalk through town, I realized something; I didn't have a clue where I was going.

"Excuse me," I stopped a man who was walking by. He turned around, surprised. It was the man with the bow tie. The one who had been talking to the guy with the sheep when we first drove in. I almost didn't recognize him without a hat. He was mostly bald, but had little wisps of white hair on the back and sides of his head.

"Yes?" he asked.

"Oh...uh..."

"Oh!"

"I was, uh, looking for something."

The man raised his eyebrows at me.

"I'm needing a place to go, but I'm not sure where."

"Well," the man said, stroking his white beard. "I think the best place to go, when you don't know where to go, is in a book."

"Huh?"

He chuckled, keeping his mouth closed as he did so.

"I own a bookshop just down that way," he said, pointing. "I was on my way to open up before getting stopped by a young, lost traveler. Care to join?"

"Oh, um..."

"I also have coffee and muffins."

My stomach growled loudly.

"And maybe I'll bring out the cheese and crackers as well," he added.

The man stuck his hand out to me and smiled.

"Archie."

"I'm Abby," I said, shaking his hand.

"Abby," he said kindly. "It is a pleasure to finally meet you. Abby's short for Abigail, yes?"

"Yeah," I said reluctantly. "But I don't really like my full name."

"Middle name wouldn't happen to be Poppy, would it?"

I stared at him and he laughed. He started walking and I followed.

"Actually, yeah. It is. How did you-"

"I'm an old friend of your grandparents."

"Wait," I said. "You know they're my grandparents?"

"Well, yes."

Archie stopped and looked at me with sad eyes.

"You don't know who I am, do you?"

I slowly shook my head. Archie grunted and scratched his balding head.

"You knew who I was when I waved at you in the car, didn't you?" I asked him. He nodded.

"Why didn't you wave back?"

"Because I couldn't believe it was really you. I saw you and your sister in the back of that car and I knew immediately."

"Who are you? Really?" I asked, stopping as we reached the front door of his shop.

Archie sighed.

"What do you know about your mother?"

11

"Which mother are you referring to?" I asked.

"Your biological mother," Archie smiled, "Olivia."

My mouth opened to say something, but nothing came out. I followed him inside the bookshop and he gestured toward a small table. I sat down and watched him start making a pot of coffee.

"How do you know- *did* you know my mom?" I leaned on the table.

Archie pulled his wallet out of his back pocket and took out a picture before handing it to me. It was of a boy holding up a fish in one hand, and a fishing pole in the other.

"Whoa," I said. "He looks just like my sister Jo when she was that age. They could have passed for twins more easily than Jo and me."

"Actually, twins run on our side of the family," Archie laughed. "Your mom dated a boy named Will. Will was my son."

I looked up from the picture.

"Will is your dad."

The words weren't registering.

"What?" I shook my head.

"Olivia and Will dated in high school and were head over heels in love. They were seniors planning their wedding while also preparing for college. Everyone thought that they were too young to know what true love really was. They didn't like that too much. So, they decided to get married as soon as my son returned from Iraq. Well, until the day he left, they spent practically every moment together. My wife, Tessa, wasn't crazy about our son coming home late every night from running around with a girl. We were afraid things were going on between the two. So, we confronted Will about it. He was always honest with us, so we believed him when he said that they were planning on waiting. It turns out, not too long after that discussion, we get a call from

Olivia's folks, your other grandparents. Olivia hadn't come home and they were getting worried. I told them that Will hadn't come home yet either. My wife and I decided to drive over to the Murray's home and wait for Olivia and Will."

I sat there, listening intently.

"Sure enough, half past midnight, we hear footsteps walking up to the front door. Charles ripped the door opened, screaming and carrying on, 'Where have you been? Do you know how worried your mother and I have been?' Meanwhile my wife and I just sat there, waiting for Will to explain. He was in shock. Couldn't speak. Olivia, very calmly, walked into the middle of the living room and waited for everyone to get quiet and listen. She told us that they both had something they wanted to tell us. I knew right then what she was going to say."

"That she was pregnant?" I asked.

"Right. I thought poor Poppy was going to faint when we were told the news. She started blubbering while Charles wouldn't even look at anybody. Will looked over at my wife and I, waiting for us to say something. Neither of us did until we got into the car. We were driving home when Will mumbled, 'I'm never going to leave her. She's my everything. We made a huge mistake that we'll have to figure out. And we'll manage, with or without your support. But It would be a little easier with it.' We didn't say a word. We didn't talk to him for a few days. We couldn't. We thought we failed him as parents.

"As the pregnancy went on, Will started spending even more time with Olivia, taking care of her, getting her going out in the wee hours to get her a Curly Wurly, talking to you two in her belly. He had matured a lot in a very short time span. His schoolwork also began to suffer though. I guess that's why he thought enlisting was the best choice. He went to basic training instead of finishing high school. When he came home from basic training, your mother had graduated, found out they were having twin girls, and was here long enough to help her name you two before getting shipped off to Iraq."

Archie started to tear up and he cleared his throat.

"Shortly after you were born, about three or four months, Olivia went missing. It was on a Sunday that your grandparents last saw her. She had taken you and your sister upstairs to your rooms and slipped out the door before anyone noticed. A missing persons report was made, and then reality sunk in. Poppy and Charles didn't know what to do. They were absolutely hysterical. We didn't know how we were going to tell Will. And then..."

Archie's voice cracked as he sat down.

"We were notified that Will had been killed. The details aren't important right now, but just know that your father died fighting against terrorism. He died without ever knowing your mum died. And, as cruel as it was that they both died so young, they were both saved from the agony of losing one another."

I sat there, waiting, wanting to hear more.

"Can I ask you something?" I murmured.

He nodded.

"Did my dad love my sister and me? You said that he told you they had made a huge mistake. So I wondered if he loved us or regretted us."

"Honestly?" he asked.

"Yeah. Honestly."

"I think he loved you more than you'll ever know. Joanna was named after my mother. She was a child while living in the Lodz Ghetto after the Nazis invaded Poland. She was the only surviving member of her family to come out of the war and eventually immigrated here where she met my father. It's funny because Joanna comes from the Hebrew name, Yohannah, which means, 'God is gracious.' Knowing my mother, you would have never known the horrors she saw as a little girl. She was always so grateful to God for everything. You both have very good, strong Hebrew names."

I sat there, completely engulfed by what he was telling me.

"You were the first one I held, you know. I remember holding you so gently, afraid you would break like a glass doll. I told your mother that your name should be Abigail, since it means, 'my father's joy.' It suited you because he was so excited to become a dad."

I had only known the man for about thirty minutes, but I already felt so much admiration and adoration for him. Fresh tears streamed down my face as Archie pulled out another photo from his wallet. It was my dad in his military uniform.

"Yes, he was crazy about your mom, and yes, he did feel terrible for putting your mom in a situation like that, but did he think you two were the mistake? No. He thought of you more as two miracles. He loved you both very, very much. And I know, without a doubt, that if he had lived, he would have taken you both in a heartbeat and raised you."

"My mom was killed. She didn't just go missing or run away. She was murdered by a man who lived around here."

"How do you know?" he asked.

I took a deep breath before answering him.

"She showed me."

"Who showed you, darling?"

I gulped.

"Olivia."

I waited for Archie to start yelling at me or tell me to leave, or even to laugh in my face, but instead he leaned back in his chair and blinked hard.

"I'm sorry, what did you say?"

I let out a long sigh.

"Ever since we arrived here, I've been seeing visions-flashbacks of what happened. Also, my mom has been talking to me. As a...ghost."

"Um," Archie started. "Well, I wasn't expecting that."

"You mean, you believe me?" I asked, surprised.

"Why wouldn't I? You don't have a reason to lie to me. What could you possibly gain from telling me something like that?"

"True, but you just met me."

"Ah, yes. But I know you. And you are Poppy's granddaughter, after all."

"Meaning?"

"Oh, one of the many reasons my Tessa had such a hard time accepting that your parents were in love was because of Poppy. There were always whispers of the witch who moved here from Ireland with her two daughters. One of those daughters moved to America. One of them stayed here to woo the young men of Surrey and to cast spells on anyone who got in her way. When she enchanted one of the foolish young men and married him, she had a daughter of her own. One who would dance around in the forest barefoot, conversing with the animals and whispering to the trees. When that beautiful young witch caught Will's eyes, Tessa was convinced that she had bewitched him."

"Well, she wasn't completely wrong," I smirked. "And I seem to have the same gifts. And Jo does too, in her own ways."

Archie chuckled lightly.

"Tessa was not an unkind woman. I want you to know that. She was only a mother who loved her son so much, she had a hard time believing that Olivia could come close to loving him as much as she did. But she would have loved you girls just as much as she loved our boy."

"Did you two ever think about taking us when our mom died?" I asked.

"We had been discussing it with Poppy and Charlie when we received news about Will's death. Your parents had specifically named Maggie as your caregiver if something should happen to your parents. We didn't want to put that on such a young girl. But then Tessa had a stroke. The stress of everything was too much. She needed my care, which meant I couldn't care for two babies on my own. I'm so sorry."

"It's okay," I muttered. "So, what happened to her?"

"She passed in 2010."

"I'm sorry."

"By the time she passed, I was just relieved to see her no longer in pain. I cared for her as long as I could, but she had to be moved to a home where she could receive around-the-clock care. I'm just sorry you never knew her."

Archie smiled sadly at me.

"You and your sister lost both parents and a grandmother. You were moved across the ocean from me and your other grandparents to live with two kids who didn't know what they were doing. And from what I understand, Maggie lost her mother around the same time I lost Tessa, correct?"

I nodded. Archie sighed and shook his head.

"What exactly has she shown you?" he asked.

"Huh?"

"Olivia. You said you've had visions and that she talked to you. What about exactly?"

I told him all of the visions I had had since the plane ride here, the meetings with my mom, and the investigation in the attic that led to me finding mine and Jo's birth certificates.

"Did you tell anyone about it?" he asked.

"Jo and my-uh-Callum."

"Who's Callum?"

"The boy I'm kind of...seeing," I explained.

"Gracious, Abby. Haven't you only been here for about a week?"

"I, uh-"

"Please, child, don't get swept away in the idea of young love. Especially after all you've learned since arriving here."

"Oh, um, don't worry," I laughed nervously, "he's a nice guy and completely respects me."

Archie let out a "mmm." I picked at my fingernails anxiously. I had just met the guy and he was already lecturing me about boys.

"Did you tell anyone besides those two?" he asked.

I shook my head.

"Not really. I tried telling my family that the house was haunted, but I didn't know she was my mom at the time. Just that it was Poppy and Charles' daughter."

"What did they say?"

"My mom- I mean, *Maggie*- slapped me and my grandma started freaking out. They didn't react too well, I suppose."

"People don't usually respond to that kind of stuff too well, especially if it's someone they were close to. Do you, uh...sense Will here with us?"

I sat there for a moment and looked around. I shook my head slowly.

"Sorry," I said.

"It's quite alright," Archie replied. "It means his soul is at peace. I'll pray for your mother's soul to be at peace. That way she can go home to Will finally."

Archie reached his hand out across the table. It landed on top of my hand. I looked him in the eye.

"Speaking of going home," he smiled. "You should go back to the house. They'll be worried about you."

"They don't need to be. I can handle myself. Besides, I have something to take care of first."

"Charles said you were the feisty one the last time we got together to play cards," Archie chuckled.

"You're the one he plays cards with?"

He nodded.

"So Jo's met you without even realizing who you are."

"But I knew. And I knew you girls would be told when the timing was right. Do you know how nice it feels to have a part of my son in my life? And for Charlie and Poppy to have a part of Olivia?"

"Do you and Charles get along?"

"Of course we do. It's funny how grief can bring complete strangers closer. I'd call Charles my best friend without hesitation. The loss of your parents and my wife broke my heart, and at first I felt so alone. But then Charles and I started talking about sharing similar feelings...well, the way I see it is, if we're all alone, at least we can be alone together. The anger and the sadness just end up weighing you down too much. I guess that's just something you're going to have to get past on your own, Abby. I read somewhere that grief is love with nowhere to go. It's all the love you want to give to a person, and can't anymore. You can go through life, hating everything and not trusting anyone

144

who talks to you, or you can forgive and live a life the way your parents would have wanted you to live. The way they would have lived."

I pulled out the book Jo had left me.

"What's that?" Archie asked.

"I have an idea," I sighed. "I don't know if it's going to work though. But I do know that I need to do it in a safe place, and probably with someone to watch over me in case something goes wrong."

"What do you have in mind?"

"I'm going to try and communicate with Seamus Harvey," I said.

"I don't think that's a good idea, Abby. It's one thing to contact someone who was a good person when they were alive. But to try and contact a murderer? An evil soul?"

"I obviously have some sort of gift," I explained. "If anyone's going to get him to confess where Olivia's body is, it's me."

I opened one of the books and ran my hand across the page. Suddenly, I felt the room begin to tilt.

"Well," I heard myself say, "here we go again."

I could smell bergamot, my favorite scent. I can also smell lavender, which always reminded me of my mother, and tobacco, like the kind my father always smoked from his pipe. I was surrounded by darkness, but at least the taste of dirt was subsiding.

"Olivia?" I heard my mother's voice call out.

"Mum?" I yelled. "Where are you?"

"Olivia, if you're here, show me a sign," my mother continued.

"Mum, I'm right here!"

"Please, Olivia, follow the light. Follow the light and come home."

Suddenly, I could see a faint glow in the darkness. I began to walk towards it and it grew brighter and brighter, until my mother came into focus. She was sitting on our living room floor, surrounded by candles.

"Mum!" I exclaimed, reaching out to her. My hand went right through her shoulder.

"Olivia, please," Mother sobbed. "Please be here."

"I am, Mummy!" I cried. "I'm right here!"

Then, a low rumbling came from behind me. I turned and saw the woods getting closer and closer to us.

"No," I whispered. "Not that. Don't make me go back there."

"Olivia, are you here?" my mother asked again.

"MUUUUUM!" I screamed as something pulled me backwards; back to the forest. I saw the candles around my mother go out all at once and she looked up, right at me. And then she was gone.

I was back in the woods, surrounded by trees. I started walking in the direction of my house, when a little girl came out of nowhere. She was covered in dirt and had a sad look on her face.

"Please don't go," she said.

"I have to get back home," I explained. "I have to get back to my parents and my babies. They need me."

"You can't," the little girl said. "They can't see us."

"Why not?" I asked.

The little girl turned around slowly. The back of her head was caved in, and dried blood caked her hair and the top of her dress. I held my hands up to my mouth and gasped. The girl turned around to face me again.

"You saw me that night," she said. "The night we both died."

"Abby!"

I felt a sharp slap across the face and gasped, sitting up quickly. Archie was on the floor next to me, looking frightened.

"Lord, Abby," he sighed. "Thank goodness you're alright. I almost called for an ambulance."

146

"I'm fine," I said groggily, standing up.

"Not for you," he laughed. "For me. You about gave me a heart attack."

Archie stood up slowly and stretched.

"Sorry," I muttered, rubbing the back of my head.

"You need to tell your parents and grandparents about everything."

"I know," I said. "I will."

"I'm serious. This family has seen its share of tragedies. We don't need anything happening to you because you think you have to do this alone. You have a lot of people who care about you. And I know we just properly met, but I've loved you and your sister your whole lives. So do me a favor and let us help you figure this out."

I quickly hugged him tight.

"Thank you," I said into his shoulder.

"You're most welcome, darling. And please, stop by the shop whenever you'd like. Bring Jo too. We've only got til the end of summer."

"I will," I smiled at him before heading to the door.

"Oh and Abby?"

I turned around in time for Archie to toss something at me. It was a muffin.

"I hope cranberry is okay. Stay safe."

"I will!" I called as I walked out the door. "And thanks!"

I had been so angry at my family that I couldn't begin to understand them. They were trying to protect me. Maggie wanted to do the right thing by taking Jo and me. She tried her hardest but then her own grief threw her into depression and alcoholism and she lost her way. I knew the hardest thing to do was exactly the thing that I needed to do. I had to forgive her. I needed to put in more of an effort to understand Maggie and Dan. I needed to help more around the house and try harder to make us a family.

My phone vibrated in my pocket and I took it out to see there was a message from Callum. He had sent me an address and told me to meet him there as soon as possible.

On my way right now.
I sent my reply before sending another message.

What's the address to?

He responded immediately and my heart started racing.

Seamus Harvey's house.

12

I knew I should have gone straight back to Poppy and Charles' house, but the opportunity to go to Seamus' first couldn't be passed up. This was my chance to contact him and see if I'd be able to get more information about my mother. The walk to Seamus Harvey's house took a little under an hour. I knew I had found the right place when I saw Callum's bike parked outside. I cautiously approached the front door and knocked.

"Hello?" I called. "Callum?"

I glanced around at the tall grass in the front and even though my sun baked skin was warm and damp, I suddenly felt cold. I pulled my phone out to message Jo but heard heavy footsteps approaching from the other side of the door. I sent Jo a blank message right as the door opened and Callum's face appeared from behind it.

"Hey," he said.

"Hi," I replied. "Why are you-"

"Come on in," he ushered me through the door.

"Callum," I tried again," how'd you get inside his house?"

Callum pulled something shiny out of his pocket and waved it.

"I have a key."

I looked at him, confused.

"Remember when I told you that Rachel and I were savin' up money for our own place? Well, this is it. This is the house we bought. I've been comin' here whenever I get free time to clean and renovate. I didn't know how to tell you after you told me everythin' about your mom."

"You bought the house of my mother's murderer..." I uttered.

"I didn't know that at the time," Callum gritted his teeth. "But I didn't want to keep lyin' to you."

I looked around at the peeling wallpaper and the thick layer of dust that coated everything. I felt uneasy.

"I thought you'd be able to maybe contact him," Callum said.

"I don't know, Callum," I breathed heavily. "I have a really bad feeling about being here."

"That's good, right?" Callum asked. "That means you can sense him?"

"I, I'm not sure."

"Well, are you even tryin'?" he asked sharply.

"The police searched the house and never found anything," I said. "I don't think being here is such a good idea. I want to go home."

"What's with you, all of a sudden? Why are you bein' like this? I thought you wanted to help your mom?"

"I do," I said, pulling out my phone. "I think I just need to let someone know where I am, in case-"

I looked up at Callum's face, which had gone cold.

"In case, what, Abby? Do you think something bad is going to happen to you? Do you think I'm goin' to do somethin' to you?"

"Of course not," I tried to say calmly. "I just think I should at least let Jo know where I am since she thought I was going back to the woods."

Callum took a step towards me and I backed up. He frowned.

"I need you to contact Seamus Harvey, Abby. I need to know why he did the things he did."

"Why do you care?" I asked. "Who was he to you?"

"No one, thanks to your mother!" Callum snapped. "He was so careful with the other ones. Never did them close together. No one suspected anything until your mom went missing."

I looked around for anything I could use for a weapon, but the house was empty. The front door wasn't too far from me. And Callum hadn't fastened the chain lock at the top. If I could throw him off guard, maybe I could make a run for it and scream for help. Had I noticed any houses close by? Noticed anyone outside or cars in driveways? I hadn't been paying close attention. But surely Callum wouldn't hurt me. He had no reason to.

"When the police searched the house, his wife grew suspicious. She got a little nosey and confronted him. Said she was going to the police and taking his son and daughter away. He didn't like that. So he waited until his kids went off to their nanny's house for the day, and tried to kill his wife before killing himself."

My eyes widened in horror.

"Yeah," Callum sneered. "Your mother was the last victim of my father, Seamus Harvey. And no one mourned for him because he died being known as the man who tried to murder his wife. His secrets died with him and Rachel and I were shipped off to live with our mother's parents, taking her maiden name. But when I turned eighteen, this house became mine, along with the land my father owned. Land that the police didn't know to search."

Suddenly, my mother, Olivia, appeared behind Callum and I jumped.

"He knows where the bodies are, Abby," she said. "You have to go with him. Pretend you're talking to his father."

Callum whipped around to see what I was looking at.

"What is it?" he asked. "What do you see"

"I, I see.." I stammered. "I see a man."

Callum looked around the living room.

"I don't see anything!" he yelled. "Prove it! What does he look like?"

I thought back to when Olivia showed me Seamus in all of the visions.

"He looks like he's maybe in his early to mid-thirties. He's huge, over six feet tall. He has black hair with a little bit of white on one side. Dark features. Dark eyes."

"Oh my god," Callum gasped, looking where I was. "It's him. Is he saying anything?"

"It's hard to understand," I said, trying to think quickly. "He wants to know what we're doing here."

"Well, I was hoping he would want to meet his son."

"He, uh, wants you to take me to where they're buried," I lied. "And then he'll show himself to you."

Callum scowled.

"Are you lying to me, Abby?"

"No!" I cried. "He wants to explain everything to you, but thinks that would be the best place to do so."

"Ask him this for me," Callum said. "What flowers did I bring to his grave when Rachel and I first came back here?"

"He's testing you," Olivia said.

"He doesn't know what kind of flowers you left," I said. "Spirits aren't always where they're buried."

Callum started laughing.

"You really think I'm that much of a fuckin' idiot, huh?"

"I, I don't-"

"He's not really here, is he?"

"He is!" I insisted.

"No, Abby, he's not. You're lying."

"I wouldn't lie to you," I cried, mouth quivering.

"Oh, you are, sweetheart. You see, my dad wasn't ever buried. He was cremated."

"RUN, ABBY!" Olivia screamed.

I turned on my heels and ran as fast as I could to the front door. I pulled on the handle and realized Callum had locked the deadbolt. Before I knew it, Callum grabbed the back of my neck and slammed my face into the hard, wooden door. And everything went dark.

When I came to, the first thing I noticed was my face throbbing. I tried to breathe through my nose and couldn't. If I had to guess, it was broken. The second thing I noticed was both wrists were tied tightly together, as well as my ankles. I was laying on my side on the hard wooden floor of Callum's childhood home. There was a fire going in the fireplace and Callum was sitting with his back to me. My phone was on the floor beside me, just out of reach. If I could wiggle slowly enough. I could call someone without him noticing. I scooched an inch and paused. Callum was too busy stoking the flames to notice me. I scooted a couple more inches and, very slowly, slid my arms and legs forward across the floor. My index finger touched the side button of my phone and the screen lit up. It was severely cracked, but I could still see the notifications. One message from Maggie:

I think you've had enough time to cool off. Please come back. We're getting worried.

One message from Jo:

Abby, where the hell are you? Everyone is worried about you. And Rachel has no idea where Callum is either. You're starting to scare me.

The last message was from Sarah, my friend from back home:

OMG ABBY! I cannot believe I haven't been able to talk to you this whole time. I dropped my phone in the pool and just got a new one. I hope you're having the best time and cannot wait to hear what you've been up to. I can't wait to tell you all about...

But that was all I could see of the message. The screen went black and I extended my finger again, this time with my thumb stretching as far as I could make it go. As I tried to grasp the phone, I thought back to my last message to Sarah.

"I'm leaving my big, American city to have fun in the English countryside," said no one ever.

I tried scooting slightly closer to my phone and as I did so, the wooden boards under my weight creaked. Callum turned quickly and I closed my eyes, laying perfectly still. I felt movement right in front of my face and a slight breeze from Callum moving away from me. I opened my eyes ever so slightly and saw that he was back in front of the fireplace. With my phone. I saw his arm jut forward and my phone flew into the flames. After my phone, he added the pagan books Jo had brought me earlier in the day, the papers from my mother's box, and the notepad. The last thing he threw into the fire was my sketchbook. He had stolen it, probably when he and Rachel came over for dinner. He got up and I closed my eyes again. Then, I felt his hot breath against my face before sudden pressure on my nose. I let out a cry and moved my head back.

"Oh good, you're awake," he said softly. "Time to go."

"Where are you taking me?" I asked, sounding like I had a stuffy nose.

"Where you wanted to go," he smiled.

"Someone will come looking for me," I cried.

"Oh, I don't think they will."

"HEEEELP!" I screamed.

"SHUT UP!" Callum yelled before pushing on my broken nose again. I kept screaming until I realized he was stuffing some sort of cloth into my mouth and then tying it tight. I gasped for air until I tried breathing through my nose again. I could hardly get enough oxygen, and my screams were muffled. No one would be able to hear me.

Callum pulled me up to my feet by the rope around my wrists.

"Go," he said, pulling me towards the kitchen.

My feet shuffled inches at a time. There was a back door in the empty, dark kitchen. Callum swung it open and dragged me towards it. Outside was a fenced in yard, however, portions of the fence were rotten or knocked over. Callum pulled me along in the dark towards a part of the fence that was completely gone. Behind it were dense trees. We were heading into the forest. I focused all of my energy on breathing and trying not to fall. Callum was losing patience with how slow I was, so he would occasionally drag me a few feet before propping me back up to walk. I looked down at the ground and every few feet or so, I noticed a flat stepping stone on the ground. It was a path.

"My father's father owned a portion of this land," Callum breathed heavily as we walked. "He sold most of it when times got rough for the family, but my father kept a small plot for himself."

In the distance, I could hear running water. The stream must have been close by. I was starting to breathe heavier from the walk, and it was almost impossible to breathe through the thick cloth or my nose. When I felt like I was on the verge of passing out, we came to a clearing full of bushes. Each bush had huge, fluffy pink flowers on them.

"They're peonies," Callum explained as we stopped. "There are twelve bushes total. And do you know what's underneath each bush?"

And then, there they were. Standing beside each bush was a little girl. Twelve girls who went missing and were never seen again. They all looked at me with sad, dark eyes, and I couldn't do anything to help them. I wondered where my mom was, or why Callum couldn't see them at all.

"My dad had an anger issue," Callum continued. "He never once laid a hand on me or my sister, and up until that last night, my mom. But my grandparents told us that he had gotten in trouble a lot as a boy. Was in fights often, and got arrested once for pullin' a knife on someone. Who knows how long this would have gone on. He might have gotten away with all of it in the end. But my father shot himself because he was afraid he'd be caught. I'd rather him be alive and rottin' in prison, but because of that...*whore*, I'll never see him again."

He turned to me.

"And as payback, your family will never see you again."

I tried to yell, "no," but it was no use.

Callum walked away from me and pulled his phone out. I started crying and pleading with him. He quickly walked back to me and punched me in the stomach, knocking the wind out of me.

I folded on the ground and tried to stay conscious. The little girls continued to stare at me.

"Rachel?" I heard Callum say in a fake hysterical voice, "I can't find Abby anywhere! She was beside herself with the news about her parents and just kept sayin' she couldn't handle it. She said she was runnin' away and when I tried to talk her out of it, she took off! I've been trying to call her but her phone just keeps goin' to voicemail! I'm so worried about her, Rach. Okay. Yeah, okay. Please do. I'll keep searchin' for her. That's fine. Go be with Jo. I'm sure they're all as worried as I am. Okay. Talk to you soon."

Callum put his phone away and turned to me, smiling. He bowed multiple times and waved to a pretend audience.

"And the best performance goes to...me!" he called out.

I was shivering as Callum approached me, bringing me to my feet again.

"Let's get on with it then," he smiled.

We came to the stream and I began to struggle. Callum slapped me across the face, hitting my broken nose again. I tried to gasp, but the cloth in my mouth was now soaked with fresh blood, making it even harder to breathe through.

"Oh, I almost forgot!" Callum exclaimed. "I have somethin' for you!"

He pulled something small and shiny out of his pocket and put his hands around my neck.

"My dad kept a few things down in the cellar. If you didn't know what you were lookin' for, it just looked like family keepsakes. But they were his trophies. And I happened to find your mother's locket."

He fastened it and moved my hair out of the way.

"Well, you don't seem very appreciative," he frowned. "I thought it'd be nice to give it to you before I killed you and buried you with her."

Without saying another word, Callum grabbed my arms tightly and dragged me over to the water. He pushed me in and my head went under until I got up on my knees. There hadn't been much rain lately so the stream was running slowly and on my knees, came up to my waist. Suddenly, he was behind me and holding my head down. I wouldn't be able to hold my breath much longer.

"Abby, you must hold on."

I could hear my mother somewhere close.

I can't, Mom, I thought. *I can't breathe. I want to give up. I don't have the strength.*

"No! Not when you've made it so far. Just wait a bit longer."

I can't.

"You can. Be strong, Abby. I'm so proud of you. You've done so well and you've helped our family more than you'll ever realize. But you have to stay alive. Stay alive so the families of the victims will know where they are."

I want to give up, Mom. I want to be with you.

"You will someday, Sweetie. Right now, Maggie and Dan need you. And Jo. And Poppy and Charlie. And Archie."

Finally, I couldn't hold my breath anymore, so I breathed in. Water flooded my lungs and it burned like nothing I had ever felt. Then, I felt the same burning down in my stomach. It was getting darker and colder. There was a distant splash and something tugged on me and everything went black.

"Congratulations," the doctor said, moving the sonogram wand away from my stomach. *"Looks like you're having twin girls."*

Will leaned in and kissed me, teary-eyed.

"Two girls," I said.

"And they'll be as fierce and beautiful as their mother," Will smiled. *"Have you thought about either of the girl names I picked?"*

"Will, I am not naming our daughters Ripley or Arowen."

"They're both strong female characters! We're having two, can't you just let me name one of them?"

"I think we should wait until they're born to decide."

"Liv, what if I'm deployed by then?"

"They won't send you anywhere that soon. Besides, I want to see their personalities before naming them. See what names suit them."

"Well, I'd still like you to consider Ripley."

I laughed at him and he leaned in to kiss me again.

"Our babies are perfect," he said. "You're perfect. And I love our little family so much."

"I love you, Will," I said.

"I love you too, Liv."

The next thing I knew I was coughing violently, water coming out of my mouth. I was laying on the ground on my back. I opened my eyes and could see the stars shining brightly above. I glanced over to see Jo sitting next to me soaked from head to toe.

"I thought I lost you," she gasped.

I looked to my right and noticed Rachel standing over Callum, holding a large branch. He was on the ground, and there was a huge gash in the back of his head.

"Wha-" I started, trying to sit up.

"Everyone should be coming at any moment," Jo said. "Lay still."

Suddenly, I threw up a bunch of water. Jo rubbed my back.

"Shh, it's okay," she cooed. "You're going to be fine. Everything's going to be fine."

"Where's Mom?" I asked, closing my eyes.

"She should be on her way," Jo said. "Rachel told me all about their dad and what happened with their mom. I kept trying to call you and you wouldn't answer. When Rachel got the call from Callum, we thought something might have happened. So I let everyone know where we might find you. And I was right."

"Abby, I am so sorry about Callum," Rachel sobbed. "I never thought he'd hurt anyone. I thought he was better than our dad."

"It's fine," I breathed.

"Abby," Jo said, "did you find out where they are? The bodies?"

I nodded and covered my face with my hands.

"There's twelve of them, Jo. He killed twelve innocent girls."

Rachel gasped and then started retching. Jo ran over to her and helped her stand.

"JO!" I heard a voice call. "ABBY!"

"We're over here!" Jo yelled.

Suddenly, Maggie, Dan, Poppy, Charles, Archie, and a couple of police officers appeared. The next moments were a blur of people around me. Callum was taken away by a couple of the officers, while two stayed behind to examine me and get statements from me, Jo, and Rachel. Eventually a couple of medics showed up and loaded me onto a stretcher. As they lifted me, something moving through the trees caught my eye. My mom, Olivia, came into view and Jo stopped to watch her too. Grandma Poppy came up beside me and placed a hand on my shoulder and lifted the other to her mouth.

"Wait," I said to the men carrying me.

Olivia smiled at us and waved. Jo waved back, which caused some confusion with the medics.

"My sweet, sweet girl," Grandma Poppy said. "I love you so much."

"I love you too, Mum," she said. "I'll see you again someday."

Grandma Poppy nodded.

"Take care of each other, girls," Olivia said to us, and we both nodded. "I'm sorry your father and I couldn't be there for you. But know that we love you both so much, and we'll always be with you, even if you can't see us."

And just like that, she disappeared.

"She's gone," Jo whispered.

"She's finally at peace," Grandma Poppy added as we all started walking.

Eventually, we got out of the woods and caught up with everyone else. I looked over at Maggie, who looked remorseful.

"I'm sorry I didn't tell you about your mother," she said.

"It's alright," I assured her. "I understand."

"No, it's not alright. You two should know about your mom."

"Well, if it's okay with you," I smiled, "I still want you to be my mom."

"Me too," Jo chimed in.

"I love you, girls. I'm so proud of both of you."

"I love you too, Mom," I said as they loaded me into an ambulance.

"I'll be right there, as soon as everyone gets settled," Dad said. "I'll stay at the hospital with you."

"I'll be okay," I said. "Promise."

"Abby, I don't want you to ever think I don't want to be your dad," he said. "The secrets have always just weighed heavy on me. But I think now that everything's out in the open, I'll do better. I'll be the dad you girls deserve. I'll be up at the hospital in a bit, okay?"

I nodded and the doors of the ambulance shut. As I was being hooked up to monitors and I.V.s, I lifted my hand slowly up to my neck. It caused a lot of pain, which I would later find out was the result of a broken collarbone, but my fingertips found the oval locket that was still on me.

"Excuse me?" I said weakly to the medic beside me. "Could you tell me if there's anything inside of my locket?"

"Sure," he smiled, carefully opening it. "It looks like two babies, one on each side."

Of course, I thought. My mother had pictures of me and Jo inside it.

"We're going to take good care of you, Abby. Just try and rest."

"Okay," I said, closing my eyes. "And it's Abigail, actually. If you don't mind."

Epilogue

My hospital stay was short, after the staff made sure I didn't develop pneumonia from almost drowning. I had a broken nose and collarbone, and one chipped tooth. The broken nose gave me two horrendous black eyes, but I was mostly upset about the tooth. After all the work to get my teeth to look good, I was going to need more work done. Although Jo told me I pulled off the "chipped tooth look quite well."

Callum was arrested after his attempt to murder me and was taken into custody. He barely spoke during his questioning, but with the evidence he left on my body and our sisters as witnesses, his charges were inevitable. Go figure the cutest boy who's ever shown me attention tried to kill me. At one point Papa Archie made a joke about the apple not falling far from the tree, but no one laughed. Callum's father killed my mother, and then he tried to kill me. Ha. Ha. Ha.

I got a replacement phone, where I was greeted with a billion missed calls and messages. The first thing I did was call Sarah and update her on my most adventurous two weeks of summer.

"And you're going to be there another seven weeks!" Sarah exclaimed during our first phone call in weeks. "And you were jealous of me getting a job. You win. And I can't believe your parents are actually your cousins! That's some soap opera shit right there! Man, if that's how your summer started, I can only imagine how crazy the rest of your summer is going to be!"

The remaining seven weeks of my summer, however, was spent helping my dad work on my grandparents' house, learning how to play gin rummy with Archie and Jo, and being taught "the ways" by Grandma Poppy. She stopped taking her medication and didn't seem to need it after the bodies were uncovered. She taught us how to garden, about astrology, and how to read tea leaves. She also helped Mom recover from her alcoholism over the summer with her "special medicine," and my mom turned into a completely different person.

Jo came out to our family, and they were incredibly accepting (although Uncle Charles did ask a few questions). At the beginning of the summer, I thought I would be the one having a fling abroad. After Callum was arrested, Rachel kept her distance from our family for a while. Eventually, she started talking to Jo again, but they agreed that they'd be better off as friends since we would be back in America at the end of summer. They kept in touch for a while, but as news of Callum, his trial, and their father's past spread, Rachel moved to Germany. She told Jo if she had any chance of having a real fresh start, they would have to sever ties.

As the summer came to an end, I was sad to say goodbye to my grandparents. I promised to call often to update them on school. Before we left, my parents gifted Grandma Poppy and Grandpa Charles a new tv. They weren't sure about it at first, but by the time we packed up our rental car, Grandpa Charles was glued to it. The first thing my mom did when we got back home was make an appointment to get my hair dyed pink again. I still wore some of the girly clothes she picked out, but I still kept a lot of my old clothes. Our time spent in England made my mom and I grow closer and more understanding of each other. I wasn't such a pain in the ass for her, and she wasn't so hard on me anymore.

My parents, Jo, and I visited every summer and every winter for a week to celebrate Christmas. Two years after our first summer, Papa Archie passed away. He left the book shop to me and Jo to decide what to do with it. Since I was already planning on going to college in England, I took complete ownership of it, while Jo stayed in America. I missed my sister and parents terribly, but I loved being closer to my grandparents.

When Grandpa Charles and Grandma Poppy died, they left me the house. I didn't change a thing about it and kept all of the furniture; although I did get rid of the books on how to contact the dead. Once or twice I thought I caught the scent of pipe tobacco or heard dishes clanging in the kitchen, but I never saw their spirits. In fact, I never saw any spirits again after the night Callum attacked me. I tried to contact my biological mother a few more times, but her spirit had moved on.

The twelve victims of Seamus Harvey were properly buried after families came forward to identify them. Other than my mother, all of them had been little girls, ages five to nine years old. The Harvey home was demolished and in its place, a memorial for the victims was put there. Twelves statues of angels holding swords toward the sky were placed in a circle, with benches and a beautiful garden surrounding them. While helping with the design, I put in a request for no peonies.

After I graduated college, I decided to move back to the United States. I felt as though my time in England had come to an end and I wanted to stay close to my remaining family. Jo got married and together she and her wife adopted three amazing kids. Love came and went for me, but I never got married or had kids, and I was okay with that. I accepted the role as the "kooky aunt who may or may not be a witch." I guess I ended up taking after my mom after all.

Made in the USA
Columbia, SC
07 February 2025

52731082R00098